"Ten years, Ricky."

"I know. Why did you stop writing?"

"Why did *I* stop writing?" She reached for her hair and scrunched it, trying to be mature. She would not bring up his queue of girlfriends that, according to the tabloids, began lining up even before her second year of college. She remembered wondering if Ricky had forgotten his promise to God.

She took a deep breath. "It doesn't matter. Water under the bridge. You have your life. I have mine. We've moved on."

"You're clipping your sentences. Apparently you're upset."

How clueless could a man be? "Do you remember who wrote the last letter?" She pointed to her chest. "Me. And that was after a long period of silence from you."

He rubbed his neck. "Look. I had no idea you were here. I don't know what to say, but obviously you do. Give me time to gather my wits." His tentative smile almost reached her heart. "You've kind of thrown me for a loop."

She could see her Ricky reaching out from the other side of the perfectly maintained actor's face. "What do you suggest?" she half whispered with resignation.

"A chance to talk—to catch up on old times and discuss the last ten years without blame."

KATHLEEN E. KOVACH and her husband, Jim, raised two sons while living the nomadic lifestyle for over twenty years in the Air Force. She's a grandmother, though much too young for that. Now firmly planted in Colorado, she's a member of American Christian Fiction Writers and leads a local writers group. Kathleen hopes her readers will giggle through her books while learning the spiritual truths God has placed there. Visit her Web site at www. kathleenekovach.com

Merely Players

Kathleen E. Kovach

Heartsong Presents

This book is dedicated to my husband, Jim, with whom I can always be myself.

My deepest thanks to the wonderful employees at the Gulfarium in Fort Walton Beach, Florida, for their helpful answers to all my annoying questions. I hope this book generates new interest for all your worthwhile projects. Also to Kim Van Meter, Film Commissioner for Mariposa County, California, and to (Tiff) Amber Miller, author and member of American Christian Fiction Writers, who helped me gain an insider's view of filming movies on location.

A note from the Author:
I love to hear from my readers! You may correspond with me by writing:

Kathleen E. Kovach
Author Relations
PO Box 721
Uhrichsville, OH 44683

ISBN 1-59789-338-2

MERELY PLAYERS

Scripture taken from the HOLY BIBLE, NEW INTERNATIONAL VERSION®. NIV®. Copyright © 1973, 1978, 1984 by International Bible Society. Used by permission of Zondervan. All rights reserved.

Our mission is to publish and distribute inspirational products offering exceptional value and biblical encouragement to the masses.

PRINTED IN THE U.S.A.

one

"Whoo-oo! We did it, Bethy!"

It hadn't sunk in yet with Bethany that they had actually graduated, and soon Hollywood High would be a distant memory. Yet, there was her Ricky, loping across the stadium, his crimson robe flapping about his body like a victory flag.

Ricky picked her up and swung her around. "We did it. We graduated!"

When he'd set her down, Bethany looked past the thick lenses of his glasses and into the forest green eyes she had come to love. The excitement she saw there went beyond the celebration of their special day.

Ricky kissed her with a solid smack. "I was going to tell you my news at your party tonight, but I can't wait."

She glanced discreetly at the healing scar on his chin. Ricky had accepted Christ in her youth group last year, but ever since the incident that had caused the ugly scar, she'd felt him pulling away. How she wished his news was about forgiveness. But she knew better.

"I heard from them, Bethy!"

"The agency?" She tried to match his excitement. "You've got an agent?" He nodded, and she hugged him. "That's wonderful, Ricky. Before long, you'll be a famous Hollywood actor."

He removed her cap and kissed the top of her head. "Naw, not without my leading lady."

She smiled. The latest school paper's headline sprang to memory. BETHANY AND RICKY, TOGETHER AGAIN. The article reviewed their final play together, *The Music Man*.

In between congratulations from family and friends, Ricky continued to share his news. "They want me to change my image, though. How do you think I'd look with dark hair?"

She wanted to answer with a vehement *No*. Instead, she scrutinized him, tousling the hair that he hated because of its nondescript hue. Was it dark blond or light brown? "I don't know; I'll have to get back with you on that one."

"Oh, Bethy," he said as he swung her around again. "Our future is set."

Bethany swallowed hard. How would she tell him they might not have a future? How would she ever say good-bye?

❧

Ten Years Later

Bethany drove the scenic stretch of highway along the Gulf of Mexico on her way to work, while light jazz music rippled from the car radio. The sights from Highway 98 between her home in Seaside, Florida, and her workplace on Santa Rosa Island in Fort Walton Beach almost always took her breath away. Emerald-tinted crystalline water kissed the sugar-sand beach with balmy waves. Feathery sea oats swayed like kites in the slight breeze while white dunes hugged their roots in an attempt to keep them grounded.

As she began her ascent onto the bridge that connected the resort town of Destin to the island, a brief weather report interrupted the music. "Enjoy the morning and early afternoon, folks. A winter rainstorm is headed our way with temperatures dropping rapidly right around rush hour."

Bethany frowned at the intrusive voice. On this warm February day, a man jogged mere inches from the waves and a sailboat bobbed in languid disinterest only yards from the shore. She shrugged. Nothing was going to spoil this lovely day.

When Bethany arrived at work, Ophelia barked at her for no apparent reason, probably just to hear the sound of her own voice.

"Hungry, girl?" Bethany threw the seal a fish treat and waved to the trainer who was cleaning the area.

She entered the fish house where she began every day at the Gulfarium. "An assistant dolphin trainer's work is never done!"

she said to herself as she chose the fish—mostly herring and squid—used to feed her dolphins in the morning. The food had already been thawed slowly in the refrigerator the night before, and she placed it into cool water to clean. Afterward, she iced it down to keep it from decomposing too quickly.

She carried her buckets of cleaned fish out to her counterparts. Four noses, all bottle shaped, poked from the surface of the water. They followed her around to the lower platform where she threw the food into their wide-open mouths. Kahlua, the young male, chattered, whistled, and clicked to encourage her to throw faster. During this ritual, she gave each a rubdown, something they loved almost as much as the treats. The strength under their rubbery, smooth skin reminded her of her human frailty.

As Bethany threw the last fish, she heard a human voice from the other side of the tank call to her in a gentle Barbados accent. "Good morning."

"Definitely a good morning, Sheila," she returned. She never grew tired of hearing the therapist's voice, with her *queen meets the islands* lilt. How she wanted to work with Sheila full time! Bethany had been involved with the training aspect nearly all her life, following her father around when he worked at Marineland in California and then later, when it had closed, at Sea World on both coasts. But it gave her a warm feeling to be able to help special-needs kids with the Dolphin Therapy Project.

"You sound chipper," Sheila said as Bethany skirted the pool to catch up to her.

Bethany spread her arms. "The sun is shining, the sky is clear, and all is right with the world."

"What an optimist! There's a storm on the horizon, you know." Sheila waved her clipboard to signal her readiness to organize the day.

"Nah, just a little rain. What's Florida without rain?"

"Are you joining us today?" the therapist asked as they entered her office. She walked over to a file cabinet and pulled out several folders labeled with children's names.

"For a couple of sessions."

"Have you talked to Simon?"

Bethany picked at her thumbnail. "I've asked him about a promotion so I can work with you as a full trainer, but he's still not too keen on the idea."

"Why ever not?" The therapist raised her dark eyebrows.

"I don't know. Something about not being totally dedicated to this as a career. He's fine with me shadowing Dad, but he doesn't think I can hack it full time." Bethany picked up a pencil from the desk and maneuvered it through her knuckles as if it were a baton. "Sure, I ask for time off for church stuff. Also there's the acting thing. He hates it when I need large blocks of time for rehearsals and then performances. But he can't expect me to live, breathe, and drink salt water twenty-four seven."

"Why not? He expects it from all of us." Sheila flipped through a folder containing information on the first child to arrive for therapy. "Tell you what—I'll inform the trainer assigned today to let you give the commands, kind of back off, and let you run the show. Simon usually pokes his head in during the first session, so if he sees how well you do, maybe he'll reconsider."

The butterflies in Bethany's stomach banged against her abdomen. A chance to prove herself. *Please, God, don't let me blow it.*

Later, in the Dolphin Encounter Building while waiting for the Spencer family to arrive, Sheila opened the child's folder and updated both Bethany and the other trainer, Lauren. "Let's see. . .Kevin Spencer. . .age ten." She perused the page. "Autistic. . .has never spoken. . .therapy program in place, but not seeing much improvement." She smiled at Bethany. "Hopefully Cocoa can encourage him. You've seen the routine. I use positive reinforcement along with the therapy techniques he's already been using. For instance, if I can get him to look me in the eye, Cocoa will do a behavior for him."

"Got it," Bethany said as she picked at a nail.

"You'll be fine." The therapist placed her hand over Bethany's fingers and squeezed.

Soon Kevin arrived with his family. Sheila introduced herself, Lauren, and Bethany, then knelt until she was face-to-face with the boy. "Hello, Kevin. We're going to swim today. Would you like that?"

Kevin's father, a nervous man, jingled the coins in his right pocket. "Are you sure it's safe? Those fish are pretty big."

Mammals. Bethany's pet peeve. Why must people refer to dolphins as fish when surely they must know better? She began the speech she'd heard Lauren say to new families. "Kevin will be seeing a pantropical spotted dolphin today. She's a smaller species of *mammal* than her bottlenose cousins in the performance arena. Also, Kevin won't really be swimming with her. He will sit on a ledge, and the dolphin will come to him."

At the pool, Sheila positioned Kevin along the side. His parents took seats in the bleachers while Bethany and Lauren slipped into the pool with Cocoa. Sheila briefly explained the reinforcement system, then asked Bethany to introduce Cocoa. Bethany waved her hand, as she had seen the other trainer do, and the small dolphin circled the pool. Kevin locked his gaze on the sleek animal. When she came back around to smile sweetly at him, he cracked a small, one-sided grin.

His mother cried. His father whispered, "Praise God." Apparently any reaction from the boy was cause to celebrate.

Sheila offered him a choice of two colors and asked him to point to the blue one. When he wouldn't respond, she asked him, "Would you like to throw a ring out to Cocoa?" His eyes swiveled toward the pool, and she asked again for him to point to the blue ring. "I know his at-home therapy uses this technique," she told his parents, "but now he has a motive." Finally, after several minutes of gentle coaxing, he lightly tapped the blue ring.

"Good job! Now would you like to throw it to Cocoa, or do you want me to? If you want me to, you'll have to look at me so that I know." Almost imperceptibly, his eyes darted to meet her gaze. "Okay. I'll do it this time, but I'd like you to try it next. Okay?"

She threw the ring to the waiting Cocoa, and Bethany instructed the dolphin to retrieve it and take it back to Sheila. "Look, Kevin," the therapist said as she removed it from the dolphin's nose. "Cocoa loves jewelry. She has a nose ring."

At Kevin's small smile, Bethany had to swallow the lump squeezing her throat.

When he finally allowed himself to throw the ring to Cocoa, in a somewhat unconventional manner—underhanded across his body—he and Sheila joined the two trainers in the pool.

"You're doing great," Lauren whispered to Bethany.

When they were done, Mrs. Spencer dried Kevin off with a towel while his father praised his efforts. Bethany thought Kevin to be a lucky boy to have such a supportive family; they seemed to want to try anything that would help their son.

"We will hope to see a marked improvement in Kevin with each session," Sheila said to Kevin's parents. "We'll book ten sessions. After that time, I'll reevaluate and see if more would benefit him. Continue his therapy at home. What we do here should make your time with him more productive."

The seeming weight that had dragged in with the Spencers now vanished, and they walked out with a slight spring in their steps.

Bethany pulled herself out of the pool and caught a glimpse of Simon leaving. Her mind flipped through the last hour. Had she done everything correctly? *Yes*, she decided. He should have no complaint.

"Bethany," Sheila said as she threw her a towel. "You did very well. I think you're a natural. Have you ever thought of becoming a therapist?"

"You're a strong advocate for your profession, Sheila." She shook her head at the absurd thought. How much more schooling would that require? She hoped her life had finally settled down. After the move to Orlando right after her high school graduation, she'd lived at home while attending college and gave stage acting a try. When her father was offered the job as senior trainer at the Gulfarium four hundred miles away, she'd shared an apartment with a friend and paid the rent by acting professionally. Her friend married, leaving her with a home she couldn't afford, so she'd followed her father once again.

She walked out of the building that enclosed the encounter pool. The sun's rays bathed her skin with warmth but assaulted her eyes. Once she donned her sunglasses, she noticed a figure waving to her from across the performance tank. Her handsome father. She couldn't leave him again to go to some university. They needed each other. She was his only child, and Daddy was the only parent she had left.

Two more therapy sessions and several dolphin shows later, Bethany searched out her best friend, who managed the gift shop.

"Are we into circus performing now?" She laughed at Cleo's strawberry curls, which hung sideways while she balanced on an upper rung of a ladder.

"Think they could use a new act out there? Cleo Delaney, acrobat and lightbulb changer extraordinaire."

"Come down from there. You're making me nervous."

Cleo made her dismount, astounding the imaginary audience. "What's up, kiddo?"

"Your husband's been gone for a month—"

"Seven weeks and four days."

"And I thought maybe you'd like to come over for a Girl Night. We could do pizza and a movie."

"Sounds great. I'll bring the ice cream." Cleo's previous exertion caused her cheeks to flush, making the freckles on her face more endearing. She continued her closing chores, chattering even while counting change. Cleo could talk during any activity. Cleo talked all the time. "Ed called this morning. I gotta get used to this overseas stuff. He was just going to bed, and I was just getting up. Isn't that wild?" With a snort, she said, "Air Force life!"

She placed the day's proceeds into a canvas bag from the bank and asked, "How did your day go?"

"It went well." Bethany started spinning the postcard rack, but Cleo shooed her away to straighten them. "I got to play full trainer during one of the therapy sessions. You know, when that little guy smiled at Cocoa, I knew I was in the right place. Simon was watching; I hope he's more open to promoting me now."

"Here, make yourself useful." Cleo handed Bethany a feather duster and pointed to a shelf housing ceramic knickknacks. "It is so cool that you get to play with the dolphins and help children at the same time. I'm jealous."

"Sheila asked me if I'd ever considered becoming a therapist." She fingered the dusty wisps. "What do you think?"

Cleo's mouth drew to the side as she narrowed her blue eyes. "So you plan on being an actress/dolphin trainer/therapist/whatever-strikes-your-fancy-next. Girl, you're going to have to make up your mind." She seized the unused duster and threw it under the counter. "You're almost middle-aged."

Reaching for a furry dolphin puppet on display, Bethany pouted. "I'm only twenty-eight. Some people haven't even left home at that age."

"Beth, you live with your father."

Using the puppet's mouth to counter the accusation, Bethany spoke slowly through closed ventriloquist lips, "It's sintly a natter oth conthenience."

Cleo dislodged the puppet from Bethany's hand. "Don't play with the merchandise. You'll get it all fishy." She put it back on its stand, making sure the head faced outward.

Sheila burst through the gift-shop door. "Oh good, you're still here. Have you heard?"

"Heard what?" Bethany said with a shrug.

"Come down to the Living Seas room. Simon has an announcement."

They, along with the rest of the employees, filtered into the theater-style seating in front of the large tank. A sea turtle stared at them from beyond the aquarium glass.

Those buzzing with gossip seemed to think the announcement had to do with a call from a movie production company.

Cleo began waving her hands in excitement, as if drying her nails. To Bethany, she said, "What if the call was about you?"

"Me? Why?"

"You're the darling of Community Theater. Maybe he saw your last performance."

"You're delirious. They don't work that way."

Cleo made a square box with her fingers and looked at Bethany through an imaginary lens. "Love it! Love it! She swims like Esther Williams, sings like Judy Garland, and acts like Audrey Hepburn. But that hair!"

Bethany self-consciously glanced around at the gathering crowd. Embarrassed, she covered her head with both hands. "What do you mean, 'that hair'?"

"You look like a sun-bleached moppet."

Bethany scrunched her short tresses, feeling it looked better messed up.

Simon had been talking quietly to those gathered around him. When he saw that everyone had assembled, he held up his hands to gain their attention. "I received a phone call from a man who works for Galaxy Productions. He's a location scout interested in making a movie here."

"Location scout?" Cleo's disappointment showed in her translucent blue eyes.

"He'll be visiting next week," Simon continued, "and I want everything spotless. He asked if he could take pictures so the powers that be in Hollywood could make the final decision."

"What movie is it?" Bethany heard from the middle of the crowd.

"*Danger Down Under*."

"Who's the star?"

"Brick Connor."

Squeals from the women masked Bethany's gasp. *Ricky!* She made a hasty retreat to her car, gulping air and muttering, "No-no-no. . ."

two

"No! No! No!" The woman's scream came from inside a helicopter as it lifted from the roof of the building. Dan ran to it, grabbing the skid just in time. He dangled over the Pacific Ocean as his black tuxedo jacket flapped in the gust of wind caused by the chopper blades. In two fluid motions, he was inside. His nemesis, the pockmark-faced Shark Finlay, grinned at him with sharp, crooked teeth, then leered at the woman tied up in the back of the bubble.

Dan kicked at his enemy in an effort to gain control of the aircraft. Shark snapped at his foot with broad jaws.

"You scuffed my shoe, Sharky. You'll pay for that."

"No worries, mate." With a gleam in his eye, Shark tipped the helicopter, causing the woman to tumble out the open door.

Dan's head swiveled from Shark to where the woman had just disappeared. "You've left me in a quandary, Sharky. Should I stay and bring you to justice, or save a damsel in distress?" He made a quick decision, grabbed the sides of the door, and placed his feet on the skid. "See you in Sydney."

After a graceful swan dive, he swam to the woman. With a single swish of the hidden titanium blade in his watch, he released her before she drowned.

She threw her arms around his neck. "Thank you, Agent Danger, you saved my life."

"You know who I am. Who are you?" They bobbed in the water, a fishing boat already chugging up to them.

"I'm Agent Risk, the rookie."

With a swarthy raise of his brow, he said, "I wish I'd known the *Risk* before I jumped in."

The scene faded with a long shot of Australia, and the words:

SEE AGENT DAN DANGER
IN HIS NEXT ADVENTURE
DANGER DOWN UNDER

Wild applause thundered in the auditorium where the premiere of the third movie in the series, *Danger on the High Seas*, had just played. Brick Connor sulked in his seat and turned to the man who had played the villain, his best friend and mentor, Vince Galloway. He leaned in, speaking for Vince's ears only, "And for this, we get paid the big bucks?"

Vince's grin showed his now-straight teeth, perfectly tucked inside his naturally pockmarked face. "No worries, mate." He cleared his throat and shifted his square body to sit more comfortably in the upscale leather theater seat. "It's going to take me forever to get rid of this Aussie accent."

"Don't get rid of it too soon. We still have"—he wiggled his fingers ominously—"*Danger Down Under* to make."

Brick had become disillusioned after the first *Danger* movie, when the company had lost their great team of writers in a contractual dispute. The second and third scripts became substandard, and the next one showed no promise of improvement. Now it was just another action/adventure film, and he was locked into a contract to finish two more movies.

Vince's wife, Evelyn, who had apparently caught his snide remark, leaned over her husband and spoke so as not to be heard by the departing crowd. "I take it you don't like the next one any better than the last."

Brick ran his hand through his hair. "I don't know; maybe I'm spoiled." He smiled at the tiny woman who nearly disappeared behind her block-shaped husband. "If I could only wedge in some meatier roles."

"You know," Evelyn said as they all stood up, "if you're interested, I've been looking for a financial partner to back the new production company I want to start."

"That's a great idea." Vince nodded his head. "She has the smarts, but we lack the funds to get it going. Could be a way to break out of your typecast."

Brick had reached the center aisle but stopped in his tracks, nearly causing Vince to plow into him. *My own production company.* He'd heard of other actors doing that, and it helped them take control of their careers. Plus, he could produce films that made a difference—that actually said something.

Vince patted his back. "Think about it. We have these location shoots coming up, but after Florida, we'll be home. Come over and we'll show you the research we've already done."

Brick's mind reeled with the possibilities.

As they were filing out, he heard a female voice talking to a friend. "I just love how they tease you at the end of each movie! This one set in the Pacific was terrific, but I can't wait for the Australian one."

A male voice answered her, "I still think the Washington, D.C., movie was the best; the first in the series usually are."

"What was that one called? I forget."

"*Danger* something. . .something *Danger.* I don't remember, aren't they all just called *Danger* movies?"

Danger Behind Closed Doors. Why couldn't people remember the title?

Not feeling like chatting with the reporters, he artfully dodged them and made his way to the limo. Neither was he in a party mood, but he'd promised some people he'd at least make an appearance.

As the car pulled away, he saw Vince and his wife talking to Bebe Stewart of *Entertainment, Now!* He noticed her looking around and knew she was searching the crowd for him. Her viewers would be disappointed if he didn't give an interview.

He shrugged. Bebe would find him at the party.

When he arrived, he perused the crowd. Several people had greeted him before he heard, "Brick-Bud! Come here. I gotta introduce you to someone."

Brick cringed. The voice came from across the sea of people gathered at the glitzy restaurant hosting the premier party for

Danger on the High Seas. It belonged to Chez, his best buddy from the early days, when partying was a rite of passage for two Hollywood bachelors. They hadn't hung out together in a while, except at social gatherings.

He reluctantly made his way through the crowd and noted with disgust that Chez wore a girl on each hip.

"Brick! This is—what did you say your name was?" The blond on his right whispered in his ear. "Oh yeah. This is Pixie, like the dust." Raucous laughter followed this announcement as if it had been a huge joke. Brick didn't get it. "And this," Chez slurred as he referred to the redhead on his left, "is the waitress. Get me some of those breaded mushroom cap thingies, 'kay, love?"

Brick shook his head as he pulled up a chair. "You started celebrating a little early, didn't you, Chez?"

"And why shouldn't I?" He floated from Pixie as if en route to Peter Pan's Neverland. Apropos, since he all but declared himself king of the Lost Boys who never grew up. He climbed onto a chair and teetered slightly as he stood on the seat.

"For I am Chad Cheswick." Chez geared up for an oration. "The greatest director in the—oops." He prefaced what was sure to be a great speech by falling off the chair and landing at Pixie's feet.

"Chez," Brick said after taking pity on him and setting him in the chair. "You were the assistant director on this film. No one cares who you are."

"But I shot some of the best scenes in that film. It's exactly what they say. Location. Location. Location." He pointed to three obscure spots in the room for emphasis.

Brick ordered a club soda for himself and coffee for his friend. "Yes, Chez. You are the best at location shots."

"Thank you. That's all I'm saying."

Although Chez was only hired for small scenes, those that the director himself didn't need to be at, Brick enjoyed working with him. If only Chez would grow up, he'd be a great director.

The waitress brought the mushroom caps, smiled, and sashayed away. Chez followed her with his bloodshot eyes. "Hey, Brick. A hundred bucks."

"No."

"Aw, come on! You're no fun anymore, now that you're a *big* movie star." He made quote marks in the air.

"I'm not interested in which of us can pick up the waitress. Keep your hundred bucks." Brick had grown past the silly game playing. Chez had not.

"Just as well." Chez sipped his coffee and made a face. "I'd win anyway. We all know who's the better man here."

Brick had a retort ready on his tongue, when a stir began near the door of the restaurant. Bebe had arrived.

Chez rolled his fuzzy gaze toward the commotion. "Your girlfriend's here."

Bebe spotted Brick, and with microphone in hand and a cameraman over her shoulder, she swept down on him as if she were a hawk snatching a mouse.

"Brick Connor, you ditched me!"

"Sorry, Bebe. I had places to go, people to see. You know how it is." He stood and greeted her with a kiss on her coral-tinted cheek.

Yes, they had been an item, back when she interviewed him for the first *Danger* movie. It only lasted a couple of months, and they broke it off amiably.

He respected Bebe's profession as a reporter over the stalking paparazzi. The latter were sleazy photo hounds who didn't care whose privacy they invaded, as long as they could make a quick buck.

Smoothing her royal blue Dior jacket, she looked into the camera. "This is Bebe Stewart with your *Entertainment, Now!*"

As she began asking questions, he tried to answer professionally, but then she went in for the kill. In a few simple steps, she had him admitting that he'd been unhappy with the last few films and was searching for roles with more substance. He kicked himself. That would come back to bite him for sure.

Maybe subconsciously he wanted the world to know there was more to Brick Connor than Agent Dan Danger.

❧

"Beth?"

Cleo! She'd forgotten all about her. "Up here."

She heard pounding footsteps, as if Cleo had scaled the stairs two at a time.

Cleo swung open the bedroom door. "What are you doing? You scared me to death." She raced to the floor where Bethany sat cross-legged. "You hightailed it out of there so fast, by the time I got into my car to follow, you were out of sight."

Bethany picked feverishly through her high school mementos, the cardboard box in which they'd been stored turned upside down and the contents scattered around her.

Cleo's heart showed through her clear blue eyes. "What's wrong?"

"That m–movie. . ." was all Bethany could squeeze out of her throat.

"What movie? What are you talking about?"

Bethany finally held up a picture she had clutched in her hand.

Cleo looked perplexed. "Beth, this looks like a very young *you* with a handsome kid, so what?"

"Look closer! See who that is?" Bethany swallowed the hysterics that threatened.

"He looks familiar. Is he someone I should know?"

Bethany rolled her eyes in frustration. "It's Brick Connor!" she ground out, shaking the picture for emphasis.

"Let me see that." Cleo pried the picture from Bethany's white-fingered grasp. "Are you sure? Brick Connor has dark hair and an incredible tan. This kid has light brown hair and freckles."

Bethany rose to her hands and knees to search in the pile further. Finally finding a magazine, she held up the picture on the cover to compare with the boy in the photo.

"I don't believe this," Cleo said. "You knew Brick Connor as a kid? How cool! But, what's the fuss?"

Bethany sighed deeply to gain control. "Brick Connor used to be Ricky O'Connell, my boyfriend in high school. He changed his looks and his name when he started acting." She compared the contact-lens-wearing Brick to her horribly nearsighted Ricky with glasses. She preferred the latter.

When Cleo leaned against the bed, Bethany's black-and-white cat made an appearance from under the dust ruffle. She rubbed along Cleo's outstretched leg.

"Hello, Wilhelmina. Were you hiding from Hurricane Bethany?"

"You know her name's not Wilhelmina," Bethany snorted, the last shudders of emotion fading away.

Cleo picked up the cat and snuggled the pink nose against her own. "Sorry, Willy. Whoever heard of naming a cat after a fish?"

"Not a fish, you dodo, a killer whale, after the movie *Free Willy*."

"Then why don't you call her Freebie?" Cleo grinned. Bethany snatched the feline and held her close to her heart. Willy purred ecstatically. "Because she wouldn't answer! Now back to my problem—"

"I still don't see a problem. You dated a boy who grew up to be a multimillion-dollar box office star. It might be fun to see him again, talk over old times, exchange autographs—sell his for a profit."

Bethany placed Willy on the bed and began to straighten the mess on the floor. "We more than *just dated*. We were semi-engaged."

"Semi-engaged is like being a little preg—" Bethany placed the palm of her hand in front of Cleo's face, thereby halting the rest of that sentence. Cleo flicked the hand away. "Well, you either are or you aren't! How can you be semi-engaged?"

With trembling hands, Bethany reached for a small heart-shaped box. She carefully lifted the lid to reveal a delicate gold band with a tiny diamond chip setting.

"He gave this to me the day I found out we were moving."

Bethany thought back to that bittersweet day. She'd waited until after the graduation party to spring it on him. Her father had decided to relocate to Orlando, Florida, and work at Sea World there. They would move the next month. Ricky had the promise ring in his pocket, thinking they'd be together forever.

"We were a good team," she said as she methodically shuffled through some old school playbills. "He was Tony; I was Maria. He was Don Quixote; I was Dulcinea. He was Professor Harold Hill; I was Marian, the librarian." Symbolically she threw her past back into the box and sealed it.

"Shortly after graduation, my father moved us across the country. Ricky stayed in California and dedicated himself to his career. His letters dwindled to a trickle. By the time Dad was offered the senior trainer job here, we'd stopped communicating." She shrugged her shoulders and ran her hand through her cropped hair. "When he became Brick Connor, I ceased to exist."

She had been so afraid her leaving would affect his spiritual life. Ricky depended on her family for guidance. Apparently she was right.

Cleo, after a moment of uncharacteristic silence, finally asked, "You mean, he gave you a promise ring, without any commitment?"

"I thought it was a promise ring. I guess it was more of a 'good-bye' ring."

"I can't believe that all this time you knew Brick Connor and you never told me."

Bethany thought of the real reason her father had insisted on leaving California. *That's not all you don't know about me, Cleo.*

❧

Finally home after pouring Chez into a limo, Brick shed his tux for a ragged pair of sweatpants and an LA Lakers T-shirt. He sank onto his overstuffed couch, reached for the remote, and placed his bowl of ice cream on his stomach. He wasn't hungry—the sweet treat served more as comfort food than anything else. Mmm. . .Choco-Mallow Swirl. At this moment, better than a woman.

Before he could find the movie-classics channel, the phone rang.

"Argh! It's a conspiracy!" He listened to the answering machine. Best invention ever. Screening his calls kept him sane.

A thick Alabama accent rolled out of the speaker and moseyed barefooted to his ear. "Brick? Brick, honey? Pick up, darlin'. It's me."

Maggie.

He picked up the phone. "Hey, Maggie."

"Hey, Brick." It sounded like an episode of *The Andy Griffith Show*. Should they amble over to Floyd's for a haircut and piece of gossip? "I saw your interview with Bebe Stewart. She worked you over, didn't she?"

"Naw, I had her in the palm of my hand." And she bit him on the thumb. "How's the album going?" When he'd first met Maggie, she had been contracted to sing in the second *Danger* movie. At that time, Maggie was a young, ambitious country singer, just coming into her own. Now, as the lead singer of an all-girl country band, she could belt out a tune that could make a coal miner weep. And she played the fiddle—never call it a violin in her presence—as good as any at Carnegie Hall.

"Recordin' simply drains me. Almost as bad as the concerts. Plus, I'm lonely. If you want to get away from the rat race there, you can join me in Nashville. It's beautiful this time of year."

Brick's upper lip began to sweat under his mustache. Maggie seemed to think she could turn him into a Southern gentleman after sporadic dating and a long-distance relationship. He had a brief vision of sitting in a rocking chair on a wide veranda, him in a white suit and her in a frilly hoopskirt.

With a shudder, he said, "Sorry, Mags, I can't get away just yet. I'm about to go on location for this next movie."

He heard an exaggerated sigh. "Well, when we're through

wrapping up this album, we'll be going on tour to kick it off. Chances of coordinating our schedules will be slimmer than a snake slidin' through a picket fence, but let's try when you get back."

"Sure thing." He looked longingly at his ice cream, melting by the minute. Time to wrap up this conversation. "Well, you take care of yourself. I look forward to hearing that new album." Not really. Country music set his teeth on edge.

"Okay. I love you."

Brick hesitated. He had never said the *L* word to anyone in his adult life. "Backatcha, babe." He hung up, mentally going through a list of synonyms that would have been far better than *backatcha*.

After about an hour, the adrenaline of the premiere began to wear off, and Brick fell asleep in the middle of an old western. His dream produced a fuzzy image of someone he had said the *L* word to a long time ago. Her father had just made the announcement. They were moving. Where was it? Far away, that's all he remembered. She clutched his ring to her chest, and he promised he would always *L* word her. Even in his dreams, he couldn't say it. The image faded, and the only person left was a teenage boy surrounded by shards of his shattered heart.

three

Ken Kirby, the location scout, showed up with his camera and focused in on every inch of the Gulfarium. Bethany watched him enter the performance area with Tim Grangely, seal trainer, hot on his heels. Tim was assigned to be the tour guide, but it sounded more like he'd assigned himself Gulfarium guardian. Thankfully, Mr. Kirby seemed like a patient man.

While he snapped away at the water, the bleachers, and the surrounding area, he informed them that only a few short scenes would be filmed of the actors running through the aquarium and shooting at each other. In the actual movie, they'd be running through a zoo in Australia.

"Since it's more cost-effective to do most of the action shots Stateside, we've chosen several attractions to film in, and we will create our own park later. You know, piecing it like a patchwork quilt." He knelt and took pictures of the mischievous Kahlua, splashing water with his bottle-shaped nose to get attention. "We only plan to be here about a month."

"A month?" Tim whined. "Won't that be disruptive?"

"We'll do all our shooting in the evening, after the tourists have gone." He further promised that all the large equipment would be set back and hidden with a cover.

As they walked away, Bethany heard Tim's objections again, followed by Mr. Kirby's professional tone. "We use computers, so no animals will be hurt making this film."

❧

A month had gone by since Ken Kirby's visit. Bethany hadn't slept well since finding out that his photographs were approved and all systems were go. She took her concerns to the Gulfarium's oldest living resident. He watched her wisely, as only a hundred-year-old loggerhead turtle would.

"How will I ever get through the next four weeks?"

She tried to think of ways to be absent during the filming. Maybe if she broke her leg. She sighed. No, then she would hurt in two places—her leg *and* her heart.

"You're so lucky, Absalom. You've got that big, protective shell. Would you let me borrow it while Ricky is here?"

Absalom opened his mouth as if he were about to give her the answer of the ages but then snapped it shut. Only a yawn.

Bethany looked up to see Cleo approach, wiping her forehead. "I know we're not supposed to have perpetual summer like the rest of Florida," Cleo said, "but our springs are hardly worth mentioning. Here it is March, and I'm already sweating."

"You're just used to your air-conditioned shop. It's beautiful out here." Bethany turned her face toward the sun, allowing its warmth to soothe her frayed nerves.

"Still, I'd rather skip summer and go right into fall."

"No! Don't rush the calendar. 'B-Day' will be here soon enough."

"Huh?" Cleo tilted her head.

"That's what I'm calling the dreaded 'Brick Day.' This is March, and after that—"

"After that—the actors attack!" Cleo came to attention and saluted sharply. "What can we do to prepare, General?"

"Retreat," Bethany said, trying not to grin. But Cleo's antics got the best of her, and she couldn't keep the corners of her mouth from curving upward. "You're so good for me. What did I do to deserve a friend like you?"

"You're blessed." Cleo's eyes twinkled with mischief. "You know, we have about fifteen minutes until choir practice. You might consider tearing yourself away from that old turtle and giving a little bit of yourself to the Lord."

"Did you hear that, Absalom? Little does she know that you're a sage, just waiting for the right question." Absalom turned his 350-pound body away from the girls. "I guess I didn't ask the right question."

ﾞﾑ

"It's really happening. . . ."

"What is that thing?"

"Glenn, if any of my animals suffer—"

"I need a grip over here."

Bethany walked through her beloved aquarium listening to the various snippets of conversation. By seven o'clock in the evening, the production crew invaded as if all of Normandy depended upon them. Cameras, lights of all shapes and sizes, generators, booms. . . She nearly tripped over a man laying tracks upon which rolling platforms would eventually be placed. Her workplace now resembled a working movie set.

How are they ever going to hide this stuff by tomorrow? Bethany moved to her station near the dolphins. Each trainer was assigned a different area near the animals. As unfamiliar sights and sounds surrounded them, they would have familiar faces and soothing voices to calm their nerves. Bethany sat on the lower platform of the performance pool and dangled her feet in the water. She talked quietly to Lani, Kahlua, Coral, and Ginger, who seemed fine but curious. They chattered and swam in circles, then came to Bethany for a reassuring pat.

"Where's that gaffer!" someone bellowed near the seals, which produced a frenzied barking.

"Keep down the noise!" Tim Grangely yelled a decibel higher. He turned to Glenn, who had joined Bethany, and said with eyes bugging, "You gotta talk to someone! If this din keeps up, no one will be in performance mood tomorrow, including me!"

"Okay," Bethany's father said, "I'll see what I can do. Meanwhile, why don't you visit all the stations and see how everyone is doing?" He winked at Bethany, and she knew he had already done that but wanted to keep Tim busy.

As Tim marched away, nodding with purpose, Bethany giggled. "I think Tim is having a breakdown."

Glenn squatted next to his daughter and threw treats of fish to four eager mouths. "Tim has a tendency to overreact, but his heart's in the right place. Personally, I think it's going rather smoothly. Once the initial setup is done, it shouldn't take long to transition from tourist attraction to movie set." He looked around at the chaos. "Remember the training film I hosted in California? At Marineland before they closed down? Maybe you were too little."

"You mean when it took Mom and me months to shrink your head back down to size?"

He splashed her playfully. "Okay, you do remember. It was a small production, but they made such a fuss. We wanted a training film and hired local college students, who were good, but not as experienced as this crew." They watched another huge light roll past them toward the bleachers.

Bethany contemplated his words. He had reminded her of Marineland. When it closed down, he was forced to take a job at Sea World in San Diego. While he was away, commuting two hours a day and hardly seeing the family, her mother had been killed in that awful car accident.

"Dad." Bethany fiddled with her fingers. "I have to ask you a favor."

"Sure, anything."

"Don't let on we know Ricky when he gets here."

"Why?"

"Remember when Mom died, and all the publicity? It will start all over again if word gets out that we're here. You know the reporters will dredge up the past."

Glenn nodded. "I understand. I guess I never thought of that. You took most of the brunt of the media. I was wrong to leave you with your grandmother in the middle of that mess."

"Oh, I didn't mean to bring it all up again." Bethany laid her hand on his arm. "I should have moved down there with you, but I selfishly wanted to graduate with my friends." She felt her lips tremble as she tried to smile. That year had been the hardest of her life. Her mother tragically ripped from her, her father abandoning her to grieve on his own—or had she abandoned him? Then the move across the country. She forced herself to brighten up. "And, hey, you've more than made up for it by letting me stay with you all these years."

"Sweetheart, you're my daughter. We should be together." He tapped her on the leg. "However, if your Prince Charming arrives, it's time you donned your glass slippers."

"So what are you saying? That I'm an old maid?"

"If the slipper fits."

At that point, Simon appeared at the railing. "How's it going?"

"Pretty good," Glenn said. "The only one who needs a tranquilizer right now is Tim."

Simon chuckled. "Have you seen that guy with the gray ponytail and wearing a T-shirt that says MAKE FILM, NOT WAR? A moment ago, I saw Tim yelling at the poor guy, who was holding the business end of an extension cord and looking at the otters. I think Tim was afraid he'd electrocute them."

After a good laugh, Glenn said, "Maybe I should send him home."

"No," Simon said. "Then he'd be calling me every five minutes to make sure the turtles were still in their shells."

Glenn stood up and surveyed the chaos. "I'll go find him—maybe give him something else to do."

As he passed by Bethany, he mussed her hair. She knew it was his way of saying, *I'm sorry I hurt you, and I love you more than words can say.*

Simon joined Bethany on the platform. "Got a moment?"

"Sure," she said as she hugged her knees.

"I appreciate your helping out this evening. I know how busy you are with all your other activities."

Here it comes; he hates my other activities.

"I've seen you helping Sheila," he continued, "and I know you'd like to do that on a regular basis. You're good with the children, not to mention your dedication." He motioned to the four gray bodies milling about in the pool.

A compliment? From Simon?

"I'm promoting you to full trainer. You've earned it."

Bethany resisted the urge to throw her arms around Simon's neck. "Thank you, Simon. I won't let you down."

"See to it that you don't."

Bethany was left alone with her thoughts. She'd be elated with her good news if her thoughts weren't on a more pressing matter. Filming would begin tomorrow. Twenty-four hours and she would see Ricky again. She played that first meeting over and over in her mind.

Coolly she looked at him. Icicles hung in the air at her frosty glance. Would he recognize her? She didn't care.

"Hello, B–Bethany," he stuttered. Apparently her rare beauty unnerved him. "You've g–grown up. . .a lot!"

"Richard. How good of you to make your little movie here."

She turned on one heel, leaving him gaping after her like a pimple-faced adolescent.

"Bethany, wake up." Cleo, who had already kicked off her shoes, pushed Bethany's shoulder while she sat down and placed her feet in the water.

"Hmm?"

"You must have been daydreaming. I stood here talking to you for five minutes before I realized you weren't listening." Kahlua gave Cleo a little splash with his nose. The other three noticed the attention and crowded around for a group cuddle.

"Where have you been?" Bethany asked.

"Catching up on some paperwork. I wouldn't miss this for anything. They promised I could stay if I laid low."

"What else could you do, shorty?" she said with a smile.

"Insults? You've got your sense of humor back? At my expense?"

"Sorry." Bethany leaned into her friend and shoved her with her arm.

"Hey, I'm just glad to see you back with the living. Are you okay?"

Bethany squared her shoulders and took a cleansing breath. "Yeah, I'm okay. It's all in the past. Ricky and I are two different people now. He will give his little performance and move on, and so will I. They'll only be here for a month. I can handle a month. Besides, it's over. I feel nothing for him."

"Good." Cleo looked at her as if trying to read between the lines. "I've been praying for you."

"Good."

"It's all over?"

"All over."

Cleo nodded as if trying to convince herself. "Then do you want to hear my news?"

"Of course! Is it exciting?"

"Not *this* kind of exciting." Cleo motioned toward a camera on a boom. The crew was blocking shots for the next day. "But exciting to me. Ed is coming home in a month."

"I thought he was supposed to be gone a year."

"This is just a visit. He left only a few days before Christmas, so we thought May would be a good time for him to get away. He's taking leave then but has to go back in three weeks."

"I'm happy for you." She gave Cleo a squeeze. "Any plans?"

"We're going to go see his folks in Vail. Do you think it's cold there in May?"

"I don't know. Isn't Vail in the mountains? Maybe you'd better be prepared. What will you do without sand in your shorts for two weeks?"

"Oh, Colorado must have something. Mud, pine needles— I'm sure I'll get into some kind of mess."

The director had promised that by ten o'clock the crew would be finished. Bethany looked at her watch. "How about that? Right on time." The equipment was hidden as promised. Tomorrow evening, filming would begin at seven o'clock and run until the wee hours of the morning.

The craft wagon brought catered snacks. The film crew and the Gulfarium employees all stood around in the snack bar area getting to know one another. The extra light that had been brought in to simulate daylight kept the evening chill at bay, creating a pleasant ambience.

The subject of Bethany's acting skills surfaced again.

"Really?" the director asked. "Have you done anything professionally?" He thrust out his hand. "I'm Chad Cheswick.

My friends call me Chez."

She shook hands and introduced herself. "Mostly I performed at the Orlando Shakespeare Festival and in repertory theater here and there. Now it's more of a hobby."

"Have you ever considered moving to Hollywood? You could make it big in film."

"Oh no. We lived in Los Angeles years ago. I'm not ready to go back." She felt sweat break out on her upper lip. No way was she moving back. Even though she fought it at first, her father had made a good decision, and they never regretted it.

Chez interrupted her thoughts. "Why would you deny the camera's eye from immortalizing that lovely face? I can tell you're very photogenic."

Cleo broke away from another conversation. "Bethany's talents are invaluable here. Not only is she an accomplished dolphin trainer, she also sings in the choir at *church*."

Bethany rolled her eyes.

Chez folded his hands in front his chest. "You know, we need more good, moral people in our profession."

Cleo's eyes narrowed, and Bethany nudged her before she could make another comment. She found herself warming to Chez. Not bad-looking, either. His dark hair hung in stubborn wisps over his cool blue gaze. Yes, very attractive. A little short, but easy on the eyes, as her grandmother would say.

Bethany noticed that most of the crew had dispersed to finish what they were doing before the break. Chez turned to answer a question from a man with a cable coiled over his shoulder.

Cleo grabbed Bethany's elbow and whispered, "Something about this guy makes me want to wash my hands."

"Don't be silly. He's just being polite."

The angle of Cleo's mouth suggested she felt otherwise.

Chez took Bethany's arm and steered her away from the crowd. "So, what church do you go to?"

Cleo began to follow, but Sheila ran up to her.

"Cleo," she said breathlessly, "my car won't start, and I need to get home. Can you give me a ride?"

"Again? You need to ditch that antique." She gave Bethany a warning look that said *Don't let yourself be alone with this guy.* But what she said was "Call me later."

Simon entered the area and thanked his workers for a job well done. "You may all go home. I'll see you in a few hours." Everyone groaned. Bethany wanted to leave, too, but she and her father had come together that morning.

She turned to Chez and held out her hand. "I'm sure you're busy. It was nice meeting you." He surprised her by latching on and leading her to a table.

"Actually, I'd like to hear more about Bethany, the actress."

She politely sat with him, worried that she was keeping him from something important.

After a moment's thought, she said, "Our community theater will be presenting *As You Like It* in the fall. Since my training is in that genre, I'm excited because it's the first Shakespearean play we've attempted."

"What other things have you done?"

After reciting her résumé, she moved on to her role as dolphin trainer.

"How did you get into that from acting?"

"Just following the family business." She elaborated by telling about her father.

Before she knew it, they'd talked for nearly an hour. He seemed quite pleasant. She'd have to tell Cleo she was wrong.

"It's been a pleasure, Bethany Hamilton, local actress and dolphin trainer." He reached out and wrapped both of his hands around hers, stroking her palm with his thumb. "You know, Florida can't afford to lose you." He leaned in, piercing her with those blue eyes. "I'd love to get to know you better. Think you might find some time while I'm here?"

It might be good to have Chez as a friend. Keep my mind off you-know-who.

While nodding her assent, she made the mistake of looking over his shoulder. A new player entered stage left: tall and suave Brick Connor.

four

Ricky!

Chez had turned to follow her gaze. He looked back at her, a broad smile on his face and a gleam in his eye.

He turned and called out, "Hey, Brick-Bud."

Ricky—Brick—Ricky. . .*Oh, what should I call him now?*— who had been greeting some of the crew, turned at the sound of Chez's voice. Bethany immediately looked down.

"Don't be shy." Chez tugged gently and pulled her to a standing position. "Brick's a nice guy. He doesn't bite—hard."

He draped his left arm reassuringly over her shoulders and led her forward. The men shook hands.

"How was Australia? Did you meet any sheilas?"

"If you're referring to kangaroos, only in the Taronga Zoo." Ricky's voice had matured and seemed to take on a sarcastic quality. However, it still melted her insides.

Throughout the exchange, Bethany stood with her hand half covering her face. She must look like a starstruck ninny.

She didn't dare take in the full effect of Brick Connor, as if he were Medusa and could turn her to stone. She tried to focus on his boots, no doubt straight from Italy, but with a will of its own, her gaze drifted upward. Jeans covered lean legs that had done their own stunt work. A manicured hand disappeared into the front pocket, pulling the suede jacket to one side revealing a black button-down shirt. Through splayed fingers, she ventured a peek at the strong chin she remembered so well, a faint hint of the scar still there. Lips. *No, skip the lips.* The actor's trademark mustache, dark under the small but slightly bulbed nose, revealing his Irish heritage. . . She would have to look into his beautiful forest green eyes. No, she would rather jump into the dolphin pool with weights on her ankles.

She felt a squeeze on her shoulders, and Chez said, "Brick, I would like you to meet Miss Bethany Hamilton. Bethany, this is Brick Connor."

Bethany slowly lowered her hand from her face. She looked up, and disappointment washed over her when brown—not forest green—contact-shrouded eyes blinked in surprise. Before he could say anything, she thrust her hand toward him.

"Mr. Connor, we're honored to have you here."

∂&

Bethy?

If he'd known she was here, he would have polished his boots and probably wouldn't have pulled his jeans from the bottom of the hamper. *And this jacket!* How long had he owned it? Good thing she couldn't see the hole in the lining. Speaking of holes. . . There was a gaping chasm in the pocket of his pants. With all the suaveness he could muster, he felt inside for his change. At least the shirt was new.

Apparently she wanted to keep their knowledge of one another private. Shaking her hand, he nodded. "It's nice to meet you, Miss Hamilton."

He noted the territorial arm draped over her delicate shoulders but resisted the urge to punch good ol' Chez right in the nose and wipe away that Cheshire cat grin.

The grin continued talking. To the untrained ear, one would have thought the conversation cordial enough. But Chez's voice dripped with oily sarcasm that only Brick could hear.

"Bethany," *who I saw first,* "is a dolphin trainer here," *where I spotted her.* "Plus, I hear she's quite the little actress." *I've gotten to know her, and I want to know her better.* His smirk communicated: *One hundred dollars if you can take her away from me.*

Clearly, Chez wanted to make Bethany a part of the game.

∂&

As Chez droned on, Bethany's eyes locked with Ricky's. Memories volleyed back and forth. If they had been observable, they would have played like a teen flick. She clutched her hair, knowing he'd noticed she'd cut it. He rubbed the scar on his chin with his knuckle—neither would forget that night. When Ricky sent her a smoldering silent message, she knew he was thinking of their intimate moments. She felt the blush rise up her throat and dropped her gaze, breaking the silent communication.

"Hey, Chez, we need you over here," a voice called out.

She almost thought Chez was going to drag her over to the cameraman, but Ricky reached for her hand. "So, you're an actress," he said. When she took a step toward him, Chez seemed to go weak, his arm feeling like a dead fish over her shoulder. He let her go and started barking orders at the crew.

Ricky drew her hand through his arm and led her away from the activity. When they were out of Chez's view, she slid her hand away, aware of the muscles under his jacket that had developed in the last decade.

They wandered to the south edge of the park, in daylight a panoramic spectacle looking toward the Gulf of Mexico. Bethany peered into the darkness. The moon, though a sliver, reflected off the whitecaps that rolled toward the beach. A void stretched beyond as far as the eye could see.

Ricky stopped and gently turned her to face him. "Hi, Bethy." His velvet voice stroked her ear with the familiar nickname.

She dared to look up. The spicy scent of his expensive cologne swirled around her. With determination, she gained the strength to break away.

"Please don't call me that."

He jammed his hands into his pants pockets.

"Ten years, Ricky."

"I know. Why did you stop writing?"

"Why did *I* stop writing?" She reached for her hair and scrunched it, trying to be mature. She would not bring up his queue of girlfriends that, according to the tabloids, began lining up even before her second year of college. She remembered wondering if Ricky had forgotten his promise to God.

She took a deep breath. "It doesn't matter. Water under the bridge. You have your life. I have mine. We've moved on."

"You're clipping your sentences. Apparently you're upset."

How clueless could a man be? "Do you remember who wrote the last letter?" She pointed to her chest. "Me. And that was after a long period of silence from you."

He rubbed his neck. "Look. I had no idea you were here. I don't know what to say, but obviously you do. Give me time to gather my wits." His tentative smile almost reached her heart. "You've kind of thrown me for a loop."

She could see her Ricky reaching out from the other side of the perfectly maintained actor's face. "What do you suggest?" she half whispered with resignation.

"A chance to talk—to catch up on old times and discuss the last ten years without blame."

She considered his words while glancing at the lit-up dial on her watch. "It's too late tonight."

"How about tomorrow?" He looked around. "And preferably away from prying eyes." As if on cue, a flash came from somewhere below on the beach. "Well, that'll be in tomorrow's rag. BRICK CONNOR TO WED UNKNOWN DOLPHIN TRAINER."

With the flash came an unbidden memory. Bethany found herself thrown back to the day her mother died. So many photographers. So many questions. She couldn't take it again. "Impossible. I won't be sneaking around with you while all of America watches. Just do your little movie and get out of my life." She turned and stormed back to find her father.

ঌ

Brick watched Bethany's exit in stunned silence. He hardly felt he deserved that. So, she hadn't outgrown her tantrums. It was best to let her cool off. He'd be around for a while.

Ten years. Why had they stopped writing? She'd been important to him in his youth, but had maturity dimmed his love for her? By the thumping of his heart, he'd have to guess *no*.

He looked back toward the Gulf. The wind had picked up a little, drawing the salt air up the coast. His eyes stung, feeling the effects—or had Bethany's final remark sunk in?

ঌ

The next morning, as Bethany prepared the daily herring for

her dolphins, Cleo poked her head in briefly. "You didn't call me last night."

"I'm sorry; I forgot."

Her friend disappeared, then reappeared. "Well, what happened?"

"What happened about what?"

Again, Cleo disappeared. Bethany left her work and walked toward the door. They nearly collided as Cleo thrust her red head back in.

"What are you doing?" Bethany asked while clutching her heart to keep it from beating out of her chest.

"I can't stand the smell of dead fish. I'm getting a big breath of air outside and letting it out inside while I talk to you."

Bethany shook her head in wonder. "How can you work here, then? Stay out here, and I'll wash up." They walked out toward the performance pool. "What's on your mind?"

"What do you think is on my mind?" Cleo flailed her arms. "I left you with a handsome director—who is clearly interested in you, by the way. Tell me what happened."

"He seemed very nice. We talked awhile, mostly about me. Then he held my hand."

"I knew he couldn't be trusted. Then what happened?"

The actress in Bethany stopped for a pregnant pause.

"Well?" Cleo practically danced circles around her.

"Then Brick Connor walked in."

Silence. Bethany's chatty friend had a gaping hole for a mouth, and her eyes were as big as Golden Globes. She finally emitted a shrill shriek that rivaled anything from the dolphin pool. Digging in for the juice of the century, Cleo pulled Bethany to a railing near the penguin port. "Tell me!"

"We talked." Bethany looked out over the water. It was in this same spot she had told Ricky to get out of her life. She related the entire scenario.

"That's it? Didn't you ask if he'd changed at all?"

"Why should I have?"

Cleo sighed. "Remember what we talked about?"

Bethany searched her brain. Oh yes, the conversation about leaving her pity party to pray about what God wanted her to say to Ricky when they met again.

She studied her deck shoes and mumbled, "I guess I got caught up in the moment."

"What an opportunity to share your faith with the man!" Cleo never backed away from a point she was trying to make.

"Ricky accepted the Lord years ago."

Cleo folded her arms and pinched her lips. "And yet, you don't believe he's maintained his beliefs, do you?" Sometimes Cleo could be downright spooky. Bethany's father once said she had the gift of spiritual insight.

"No," Bethany admitted. "But, now that he's the mighty Brick Connor, why would he listen to his ex-girlfriend? He's made his choice, and it didn't include God—or me."

Cleo placed her hand on Bethany's arm. "The man's soul may be at stake, the one thing his money can't buy. Isn't that more important than your hurt feelings?"

That stung. "You're right." Bethany nodded and turned to look out over the water. Her back muscles tightened. "But last night wasn't the right time. I had to tell him how I felt."

"Sounds to me like you told him off. Did you tell him you still love him?"

"What?"

"I'm sorry." Cleo backed away. "I've gone too far. All I'm saying is, don't write the man off because of what he's become." She raised her eyebrows, reminding Bethany of her mother. With hands on her hips, she added, "You know?"

Cleo left her with a lot of thinking to do. Had she been too rough on him? Should she have shown some kind of Christian charity? Turned the other cheek? *No way.* She wouldn't offer him another soggy, tear-stained cheek. He blew his chance to have a life with her. But, she conceded, if the opportunity should present itself, she would talk to him again about God.

That'll be hard, since I intend to avoid the man.

five

"Heads up!"

Bethany sidestepped to avoid a rolling floodlight. As she walked to the tank, she appreciated the phenomenal organization it took to turn the Gulf Coast attraction into a working movie set. The production crew had promised to take only a month, and it seemed they would make good on that promise.

This time, a handful of people stayed to take care of the Gulfarium residents. All others, employees and local curiosity seekers, were asked to stay in the bleachers overlooking the performance pool. They were thrilled because, by doing so, they volunteered to be extras and simulate the audience at the fictitious Australian zoo.

Cleo joined Bethany on the lower platform of the performance tank out of camera shot. The four dolphins milled about the pool and, just as the night before, came to Bethany for reassuring pats and words of encouragement.

"This is a great spot," Cleo said.

"The action is going to start over there." Bethany pointed to the right of the pool. "Agent Dan Danger and the villain are going to run to there." She pointed to the left side. "They filled us in so we wouldn't be in their shot."

When Brick Connor made his appearance, Cleo drew in a girlish gasp of delight.

"Now *that's* a man," Cleo said.

Bethany scowled at her—but had to admit that the star's black leather pants and matching leather jacket set off his dark hair and mustache, making him appear dangerous indeed. And gorgeous.

"Look how sure he is of himself," Cleo gushed. "And he hasn't even started the scene yet." Another actor entered the area. "Ooh, I know him. That's Vince Galloway. He always plays a villain because he's stocky and rough-looking, but I've heard he's a Christian."

Bethany watched the two men interact. They laughed together and at one point even hugged. She smiled as her heart did a little happy dance. Had Vince been sent to Ricky in answer to her prayers those many years ago?

Both men talked to the director. They nodded as they received their instructions for the scene they were about to shoot. Each man was handed an AK-47.

Bethany leaned toward Cleo. "Those are going to be used to destroy the aquarium." She shuddered. Thankfully the guns were only props.

Cleo grinned. "Cool."

Chez called for quiet and instructed the cameras to roll. A woman stepped in front of the camera and called out some numbers; then she snapped the top of a slate.

"Don't they use digital slates now?" Cleo asked.

"On such a small shoot, they sometimes use the manual ones." *Just don't ask me how I know.* She needn't have worried. Cleo was so caught up in the action that it apparently never occurred to her how Bethany knew these technical things.

Upon the director's command, Brick Connor ran in from the side with his weapon, looking like a man fiercely determined to stay alive. He sprinted past the dolphin pool, and the director shouted, "Cut!" He motioned to the actor, and they talked a moment more. Then they did the scene over again—and over, and over.

When Bethany had just about decided she was bored out of her mind, Vince came in and did the same thing. Over and over. She looked at her watch. These two scenes had taken two hours to shoot.

Finally Chez called for a break, and everyone dispersed to the craft wagon for snacks.

"You want something?" Cleo asked as she stood up.

Bethany stood and stretched. That was a long time to sit

cross-legged. "A bottle of water would be fine. I'll stay here, though."

Cleo cocked an eyebrow. "You trying to avoid somebody?"

Bethany gave her a look that she hoped conveyed *Mind your own business.* Cleo turned and scrambled up the ladder.

It didn't do any good to stay put, however. Someone had brought food to the two actors, and they lounged on tall chairs near the bleachers in her full view.

ᶻᵃ

Look at her.

Brick could barely concentrate on what Vince was saying. It didn't matter. It was just small talk, a winding down from the shoot.

She used to be a cute kid, but the gangly teen had finally grown into her legs. *Bethy, you're a beautiful woman now.*

His heart flipped through hoops in his chest.

He turned to answer Vince. When he looked back, his jaw clenched. Chez had joined Bethany. Brick's eyes narrowed. *Back off, Chez. She's way out of your league.* A thought occurred to him from nowhere. She was way out of *his* league, as well. He shook it off. His first order of business was to protect Bethany from the wolf in director's clothing.

ᶻᵃ

While Chez spoke amiably, Bethany continued to glance Ricky's way. She wished she hadn't put him in his place so quickly. If only it were Ricky instead of Chez murmuring these senseless things to her.

His voice last night—I nearly lost it when he called me Bethy. How many times have I heard him talk to me like that in my dreams? The moment he had come onto the set that evening, she had felt the invisible cord that bound them together—a cord tied with memories, sweet and bitter. She wondered if he felt it, too, or was he anxious to make his movie and leave?

He looked as if he'd just stepped out of a magazine. Not the same eighteen-year-old kid she had dated, that's for sure! Even the camera didn't do him justice. Although Ricky had changed his appearance to equal star quality, she felt herself longing to see the teenager once again.

"Well," Chez said. "Break's over, so I have to get back to work."

Bethany smiled politely. She hadn't heard a word he'd said.

After another hour around the dolphin pool, the action moved to the alligator exhibit.

Cleo hopped up. "Let's go."

"No, I think I'll go to Dad's office and wait."

"Oh no, you won't. Filming by the alligators has got to be more exciting than this was. Come on; it's not every day we get to see stuff like this."

She allowed Cleo to haul her off the platform.

They reconvened at Fort Gator and found only about ten people had stayed to observe. Bethany looked at her watch. Nearly eleven o'clock. "How are we ever going to make it to work tomorrow morning? It'll be after midnight by the time we get home."

"What do you mean, *we*? I'm the commanding officer of my little unit. I've already made arrangements with my assistant manager to open so I can come in late." She gave a smug smile.

Again, the two actors chased each other past the man-made swamp.

Cleo tapped her on the shoulder and said, "I know that Brick Connor and Vince Galloway have just run out of sight, but who are those guys?"

Bethany glanced to where Cleo pointed. The hero and villain were sitting in chairs and drinking bottles of designer water.

"They're the stunt doubles."

Cleo slapped her forehead. "Duh! I should've known that."

Bethany realized that the man standing in for Vince didn't look much like him in the face, but Brick's double was just that: his double. Maybe he looked like him because of the angle or the lighting. But no. When he stood up, he could have been the man's twin. *Weird.*

Brick II moved to the area of filming. While a cameraman

worked over Vince's shoulder, the villain took a swing at the original Brick. Chez yelled, "Cut!" and replaced the real Brick with the stuntman. They shot it again at a different angle, and Brick II went flying, ending in a double roll and sprawling over the fenced area dangerously close to the pit. An alligator snapped its jaws as if on cue. Chez yelled, "Cut! Print!" and everyone broke into applause. "That's a wrap, folks. Let's get this stuff put away and meet back here tomorrow evening."

"Well," Cleo said, "that's that. Guess I'll go home and get some sleep."

"I've got to wait for Dad. We came together today because he didn't want me driving home so late." She glanced at her watch. "Or rather, early in the morning."

Bethany almost took Cleo up on her offer to stay at her place, only a couple of miles away, but knew her chatty friend would keep her up until dawn talking about all she had seen that night. So Cleo left, and Bethany headed for her father's office. She knew he wouldn't leave until the crew had put everything away. Simon had placed him in charge while the production company was on the premises.

She entered the office and curled up on the short leather couch. She fell asleep quickly and dreamed that someone had placed a sweet kiss on her temple. When she awoke an hour later, a thick beach towel had been placed over her body, and she smelled the lingering scent of spicy cologne.

six

Brick splashed on an extra dose of cologne. He stood in front of the full-length mirror in his hotel room, grumbling. "I've been here two weeks. Why hasn't she warmed up to me by now? What's it going to take?" Since her day ended as his began, they hadn't had a chance to connect. She'd reply to his greetings but then rush out. "You can't get away from me today, Bethy, because I intend to follow you everywhere."

He wore a Disney World T-shirt, blue surfer shorts that reached his knees, brown leather sandals, and he topped off the outfit with a straw hat rimmed with a red Hawaiian print. Once he placed the dark sunglasses on his face, he knew no one would recognize him.

He made it safely to his rented BMW and sped off to spend the day as a tourist.

After paying the admission fee, he headed for the dolphin show. Finding a place on the bleachers, he proceeded to scan the area.

Bethany entered from the side, following her father. They both waved to the crowd, and everyone cheered. He drew in a breath. His heart beat so hard that he was sure the people around him could hear.

There was his Bethy, in a wet suit, her fair hair acting as a halo around her angelic face. Her smile seemed to brighten the already-cloudless day, and he longed for her to look at him that way again.

She put the dolphins through their paces while her father explained their antics. Quite honestly, he wasn't even watching the show. Except for the part where Bethany, while on a high platform, put a fish in her mouth and the one called Ginger leaped up and took it away from her. *Yuck. And I want to kiss that mouth?* He thought a moment. *Yes, I do. Very much.*

Too soon, it was over, and she disappeared. He'd paid to observe a Dolphin Encounter and hoped she was the one doing it. Brick almost felt guilty. Maybe someday he would play a stalker and could have this experience to draw from.

He followed the crowd out of the bleachers and headed for the encounter tank. Grateful there were others waiting to watch, he slid in behind them, hoping to blend in. He hadn't counted on it being inside, however. His sunglasses would probably act as a neon sign to Bethany. He took them off, but left on his hat.

She soon entered the area with a family of three. The boy, who said his name was Steve Eberly, got in the tank, while Mom snapped digital pictures and Dad ran the video camera.

"Because our tanks are small," Bethany explained to the crowd, "Florida law prohibits the untrained to actually swim with the dolphin. Sorry, Steve. But he will touch her and learn how to give her commands."

Brick sat mesmerized. She really was good at her job. She brought Cocoa up to Steve's lap and gave some information on how the dolphin came to be a member of the Gulfarium family. "Cocoa came to us after stranding herself on a nearby beach. She had been separated from her mother and was found with a severe lung infection." She petted the little mammal and began to point out the differences between the pantropical spotted dolphin and the bottlenose dolphins in the performance arena. "As you can see, Cocoa, who is fully grown, is much smaller. She was born without spots, and was probably about thirty-one inches in length at birth. As she matured, the spots started showing up, and now she has grown to a healthy seventy-four inches or. . ." She turned to the boy. "How tall are you, Steve?"

"Five foot six—and growing." This caused a ripple of laughter.

"She is about two inches shorter than you." After a few more facts about Cocoa, she showed the boy some basic moves. Before long, he had Cocoa jumping, dancing, and chattering.

At the end of the exhibition, Brick left with the crowd,

resisting the urge to stay behind and watch Bethany talk to the little family. He heard her laughter and wished she'd been laughing at one of his jokes. He did venture near her, as some of the audience clustered around her asking questions. How he longed to reach his hand around her slim waist and draw her to him. *Patience, Brick ol' boy. Patience.*

❧

Bethany spoke a few minutes more with the family. "Well, Steve, now you know about as much as I do about Cocoa. Are you going to be a dolphin trainer when you grow up?"

Steve's eyes sparkled with excitement. "Naw, I'm going to be an astronaut."

Mr. Eberly ruffled his son's hair. "We took a tour of the Space Center on this vacation. I'm afraid the lure of the cosmos is stronger than the mysteries of the deep."

Bethany laughed. "That's okay. With Steve in space, I know my job is safe."

As the familiar scent drifted by, it tapped her senses to get her attention. She knew he'd been there, been near enough for her to catch a whiff of his cologne. It wrapped around her like a warm blanket, and she suddenly felt very content. When she glanced around the area, he was nowhere to be seen.

"Excuse me, folks," she said to the family and to the dispersing crowd. "I hope you all enjoyed the Steve Eberly show." Warm applause from the few who were left pleased her. But she had to go in search of that aroma.

She felt like a bloodhound. An old bloodhound past its prime. She'd lost the scent. But she knew it had been him. Her voice of reason tried to sway her thinking. *It could've been anyone, silly.* No—it was Ricky. She knew it.

❧

Brick peeked over his shoulder for a split second and saw Bethany looking around. She seemed to be searching for someone. Maybe her father. He pushed his hands into the pockets of his shorts and sauntered away from her.

Later, he was pleased to see her again in the Multispecies

Show, a performance that included a seal and the dolphins. This time Swisher the seal waddled up to the high platform, dangled a fish from her mouth, and fed the dolphin the way Bethany had earlier. He wondered if Swisher had a boyfriend somewhere thinking, *Yuck!*

At the end of the show, Bethany, her father, and the seal trainer all answered questions from the dwindling crowd, allowing them to get close enough to pet the dolphins. He noticed her looking around again, scanning the crowd. *Who is she looking for? Does she have someone special she thought would be here today?* That thought made his stomach queasy.

With one last round of performances, beginning with the dolphin show, he sat in the middle of the crowd and again watched his girl. This time, he tried to pay more attention.

"Allow me to introduce our dolphin family," Glenn said. While he talked, Bethany gave hand signals to each dolphin. He introduced Ginger first, the oldest and most experienced. Then Coral, the next oldest. Finally, he introduced Lani and her son, Kahlua. With each introduction, Bethany raised her right arm and the dolphins would circle the pool and leap in the air. Except Kahlua, described as the class clown. He circled the pool and then pirouetted on his tail fluke. Brick noticed that Bethany had changed her signal to a rotation of the fingers. When Glenn admonished the young dolphin for not following the examples of his elders, Bethany wagged her fingers and Kahlua clicked as if arguing. He then spit water, but he eventually did what his elders had shown him, with a little twist that Glenn said was uniquely his own.

Since it would be a little over an hour before he could see her in the last show of the day, Brick decided to scope out the rest of the attractions. Even though he'd spent every night there filming, he hadn't had a chance to appreciate it from a tourist's point of view.

He went underground to the Living Seas Show, where he watched a scuba diver swim with moray eels, stingrays, and sharks. In an educational presentation about life under the sea, the diver pointed out sea turtles, snapper, grouper, and tarpon. While wandering the grounds, Brick found the penguins, and just on the other side of the Shark Moat, he laughed at the antics of the otters.

At the touch pool, he picked up a seashell but dropped it when he saw it occupied by a hermit crab. How mortifying when a child said, "They won't hurt you, mister." The little girl allowed the crab to wander all over her hands. "Do you want to try?"

She held it out to him, but he recoiled. *Never did like those things*. "N–no, thanks. I'll take your word for it." He quickly left the area, chastising himself for being such a wimp. *Agent Dan Danger wouldn't be afraid of a little hermit crab.*

He eventually found himself at Fort Gator, where they had filmed the first day.

❧

Bethany waved her arms and whistled commands during the last show of the day. She'd already asked her father if he'd seen Ricky anywhere.

"You think he's crazy?" Glenn had said. "He wouldn't come here in the middle of the day. He'd be mobbed."

"I guess you're right." Still, she'd had a feeling he'd been watching her all day.

She was so preoccupied with thoughts of Ricky that she gave a different command from the one her father had explained. Instead of raising her arm to signal them to flip in the air, she raised both arms and pushed her hands upward telling all four dolphins to dance on the water with their tail flukes. The crowd roared with laughter, thinking it to be part of the show.

Glenn shot her a look, and she knew she was in trouble. Even worse, Simon had been watching from the side. She could sweet-talk her daddy, but Simon was a different matter altogether.

She forced herself to stay for the question-and-answer period, hoping they had a lot of questions, not anxious to be alone with her dad and Simon.

There! She smelled it again. Definitely the same spicy scent she remembered Ricky wearing earlier. Questions were coming at her from all directions, and she answered them as best she could. Finally a deep, masculine voice called out, "Are you free for dinner?"

The crowd parted, and there he stood. Despite the cool breeze blowing in from the Gulf, she felt a heated blush make its way from the top of her wet suit to the roots of her hair. An elderly woman stood nearby, holding a stuffed seal from the gift shop, probably bought for a grandchild. "Ignore him. He might be a masher." Grandma jutted her chin out at Ricky, daring him to be so bold as to speak again.

"It's okay, ma'am. I know this guy."

The old woman looked from one to the other, a slow dentured grin pulling on the wrinkles in her face. "Then what are you waiting for? Answer the man."

Bethany scrunched her hair. "S–sure. I guess so."

Everyone applauded the couple as he stepped forward.

≈

Brick led her away from the group, leaving the rest of the questions to Glenn and the seal trainer.

"How did you get away with this?" she hissed as they walked toward the offices.

"I've been getting away with it all day."

"I knew it! I tried to find you in the crowd."

Brick relaxed. So she hadn't been looking for another guy. "How did you know?"

She breathed in deeply. "Your cologne. I smelled it earlier, and I've been looking for you ever since."

"I tend to go heavy with this cologne. It gave me my start in show business."

"*Gentleman's Agreement*?"

"Were you following my career, Bethy?"

She cleared her throat and looked away. "I don't live in a cave, Ricky. I know you made commercials before you became famous."

"I'm sorry. I didn't mean that to sound so egotistical." He could feel her slipping away again. Why couldn't he keep his mouth shut? "So, when can you get away?"

"Away?"

"For dinner."

"I don't think we ought to go anywhere together. No use in starting something that neither of us intends to finish."

Ouch, that smarts. "All I want to do is talk over old times. Nothing wrong with two old friends getting together for dinner, is there?"

"I don't have time."

"But you have time for Chez?"

She stopped in her tracks, turned, and took him head-on. "That's uncalled for. Whom I choose to make time for is none of your business." She began to walk away, her pert nose stuck in the air.

"You need to keep away from Chez. He's a womanizer. The only reason he wants—"

She swung around and poked a slender finger in his chest. "Chez is kind and understanding. I like being with him. He understands me."

"He's using you. He thinks we made a bet—"

"You gambled on me?" Her nostrils flared.

Brick backpedaled. "No. See, we used to play this game, but I—"

He heard a voice call out to her from behind. "Bethany. My office. Now."

She put her hands to her mouth and blanched. He grabbed her shoulders. "Are you okay?"

"Please, just go away; you've caused me enough trouble." She pulled away from him and turned slowly. Taking a deep breath, she disappeared into Simon's office.

When the door clicked shut, he asked himself, *What did I do?*

seven

"Did you do it?" Cleo asked as she followed Bethany to the parking lot after work. Their first stop would be a fast-food restaurant and then on to choir practice at Safe Harbor Community Church located along the sound.

"Do what?"

"Talk to Ricky about God."

Bethany placed her athletic bag on the hood of her car and dug for her keys. "I. . .um. . .haven't seen him."

"You're not supposed to avoid him. You're supposed to help him get on the right track."

Bethany waved her friend off as if she were a pesky mosquito. "Hey, there's no time for that. He starts his day as I'm leaving."

Besides, a week ago Simon had warned her about not paying attention. He said he'd give her two more chances. By avoiding Ricky, she felt she was saving her job.

"They'll be done filming next week," Cleo said. "Then he'll be out of your life for good. Don't miss your chance, Beth."

A voice called out Bethany's name from the parking lot. She smiled. "Now, Chez is someone I've enjoyed getting to know. He's fun and doesn't seem to want anything but friendship."

Cleo sniffed. "I don't trust him."

"Don't be silly." She waved at Chez who was sprinting around parked cars to catch up to them.

"I'll wait for you in the car, Beth." Cleo took Bethany's keys and disappeared into the passenger side of the silver sedan.

Bethany leaned against her car and greeted Chez. "What's up?"

"I know we haven't had a chance to get away, and the company is leaving next week. What say we go out tomorrow?

I've given the crew the night off. We're ahead of schedule, and they all deserve a rest."

"A date?" She picked at her thumbnail.

"Well, more like two friends hanging out together. What do you say?"

She glanced toward Cleo's silhouette. "Sure, why not? What do you suggest?"

"Well, the buzz is that you have a penchant for minigolf. So, how about that with dinner first?" He shoved his hands into his back pockets and rocked back and forth on his heels, waiting for her answer.

"Sure, that sounds like fun." She heard a sound coming from the interior of her car. Was Cleo coughing the word *gullible*? She frowned at the rolled-up driver's side window. "I know just the place." She heard more coughing with the words "Don't do it" between spasms.

"Is she okay in there?" Chez leaned down to look in the window.

"She's fine. Just having problems with her nose lately." *She can't keep it out of my business.*

"Oh. So, tomorrow, after you're done at work?"

"Perfect. Why don't I meet you next door at the boardwalk?" She pointed toward the large wooden structure that served as picnic area, beach deck, and tourist trap. "It has some cute little shops and a great restaurant." *And lots of people.* She thought maybe that would ease Cleo's mind.

Chez shrugged. "Sure."

ॐ

"Five. . .ten. . .fifteen. . .twenty. Twenty dollars for a job well done." Brick laid the bills in the cameraman's hand and patted his back. "Thanks, Fred. You're sure he fell for it?"

"Oh yeah. I started spreading the rumor around that Bethany likes minigolf. Even got the name of her favorite place from her dad. Chez swallowed the bait like a big ol' marlin."

Brick felt very pleased with himself. "Great. Now, on to Phase Two. . ."

❧

After choir practice, Cleo followed Bethany home. They had arranged another Girl Night, with popcorn and a movie.

Cleo reached for the popcorn in the cupboard and pulled out the popper. "I appreciate you babysitting me like this. It gets awfully lonely at home without Ed."

"You're always welcome to stay in our guesthouse while he's gone." Bethany loved how her friend took over in her kitchen. With things in Cleo's capable hands, she hopped onto the counter and sat with her feet dangling.

"Thanks, but I love my little home; I just need some company once in a while."

As Cleo poured the kernels into the machine, she frowned slightly. Her mouth opened to speak, but then she seemed to change her mind.

"What?" Bethany knew full well what was bothering her friend.

"I don't want to start a fight." She placed the lid on the popper and turned it on.

"Go ahead. I know what's bugging you, so we might as well get it out in the open."

Cleo leaned against the island in the middle of the kitchen and folded her arms. "I've voiced my concern about Chez."

"Adamantly." The corn started to pop, one kernel at a time. "I don't see what you see. He's been very gracious to me, and he's fun to talk to. It's not like I'm rushing out to marry this guy."

"No, but you are going out on a date with him."

"One date, just as friends, as innocent as if it were you and me. Then he'll be going back to California where he belongs."

"I don't know." Cleo shook her head. "I can't put my finger on it, but something about Chez Cheswick just doesn't ring true."

More corn started popping, and they had to raise their voices. "I'm sorry you feel that way, but frankly, you have no say in the matter."

Cleo looked her straight in the eye. "You wouldn't by chance be using Chez to get back at Ricky, would you?"

The heated corn popped furiously and nearly pushed the lid off the popper. "I can't believe you're still harping on that. Can't I have a normal relationship?" However, she'd had almost that same idea when she first met Chez. But then it didn't sound so sleazy. She hopped off the counter and started melting butter in a small pan. "It's not like I date a lot. Can't you let me have this one moment?"

They were both silent as the popcorn reached its zenith, then slowly finished popping the same way it had begun, one kernel at a time.

When it was done, Cleo poured the hot snack into a large bowl. The aroma wafted around the room. "Just be careful, okay?"

"I'm a big girl. Trust me." She poured the butter over the popcorn. "Ow!"

"What happened?" Cleo hurried to her side.

"I touched the pan."

"Big girl, yeah." Cleo turned on the cold faucet and pulled Bethany's hand under it.

❧

Brick and Vince had just finished a scene when Chez called for a break. They all surrounded the craft wagon, where everyone but Brick loaded up on sugary, carby snacks. He grabbed some cheese squares and a handful of seasoned chicken wings and headed toward the Gulf.

While on the bench looking out toward the water, he glanced at his watch. Shooting would resume at midnight, and they would go until three. He drew in a big breath of salt air. Only a week to go, and he hadn't gotten any further with Bethany. He thought of the trick he'd played on Chez. *This plan had better work.*

Chez plopped down next to him.

"Hey, Brick-Bud."

"What do you want, Chez?" Brick asked without turning to look at the intruder.

"You looked lonely over here by yourself. Thought I'd cheer you up." He jammed the last bite of a cookie into his mouth. "You seem a little down lately."

"I'm fine, just tired of being away from home."

Chez draped his arms over the back of the bench. "Yeah, I know what you mean. It's sure a good thing I met Bethany. She's brightened up this shoot considerably." Brick squished a piece of cheese between his thumb and forefinger and pretended it was Chez's head. "Yep, got her to go out with me tomorrow night."

"I heard." Suddenly losing his appetite, he tossed his plate in the trash.

"Guess that means she likes me more than you."

"Guess so."

"You owe me a hundred bucks."

Brick stood and started walking back to the set. "I refused to bet with you, remember?"

Chez followed at his heels. "Oh no, you don't. I get the girl—I get the money. You can't renege."

Brick thought about *The Plan* and was sorry he'd intervened. What if the whole thing backfired? What if he'd put Bethany in jeopardy? Good thing Chez was incredibly predictable.

Chez's incessant bragging sounded like a dripping faucet. "Yeah, we're going to a nice restaurant, but then we're going to this minigolf and go-cart track place she likes. I think it's a little juvenile, but anything to keep her happy. She may be a child when we get there, but she'll be a woman before she gets home."

Brick snapped. He turned and grabbed Chez by the front of his shirt with one fist. "If you so much as lay a hand on her. . ."

They stood like that together, Brick's glare piercing the smaller man's ice blue eyes. At first he saw fear, but then, maddeningly enough, Chez turned into the Cheshire cat.

The director nodded like a bobble-head doll. "Oh yeah. You've got a thing for the little blond mermaid. But she won't talk to you, will she?" Chez raised his hands in victory. "Yes!

The mighty Brick Connor has fallen. She's mine—"

Chez yelped as Brick pushed him against a wall with the ease of pinning a varmint with a boulder. "If you hurt her. . ."

"What? You'll rough me up real good? The reporters would love that. Too bad there's no one around to capture *this* Kodak moment."

With regret, Brick loosened his grip. "If anything happens to her, trust me, you *will* regret it."

Sweat broke out on Chez's lip, giving Brick a small amount of satisfaction.

≈

After the uncomfortable exchange of words, Cleo and Bethany took their popcorn to the living room. As true best friends, they had aired their disagreement and were now ready to settle down for a relaxing evening. Bethany snuggled onto the soft cushions of the couch, crisscrossing her legs and tucking the large popcorn bowl in her lap.

"So what movie did you rent?"

Cleo shuffled through her big bag, the one in which she kept a change of clothes and a toothbrush, just in case she ever decided to spend the night. "Well, it's not an old black-and-white classic, but it's one I love and wondered if you'd ever seen." She continued to search. "Where did I put it? Did I leave it in the car?" She glanced around, as if it might materialize in a place she hadn't even been. "How's the hand?"

"It's fine. Doesn't even hurt anymore. I never would have thought to let cold water run on it. I was about to grab a stick of butter."

"Wrong move." Cleo was on her hands and knees now, searching under the armchair.

"Why?"

"Because, my medically inept friend," she said, sitting back onto her heels, "butter would hold in the heat, causing it to burn even more. Not to mention the salt in butter."

"Hmm, never thought of that. What about ice?"

"The sudden cold could cause more trauma to the wound."

Bethany threw a piece of popcorn in the air and tried to catch it in her mouth. When she missed, she picked it off her shirt and flipped it between her teeth. "How did you get so smart?"

"Just common sense."

Bethany watched Cleo lift pillows and rummage through her bag again. *Common sense.* Should she have used more common sense before pursuing a friendship with Chez? Was she using him, as Cleo suggested, to hurt Ricky? Had she prayed about what her role should be now in Ricky's life? *Well, no.* Upon reflection, she acknowledged being flattered by the attention Chez showered on her and angry with Ricky. She decided her prayer that night would be for God's direction and for Him to impart on her some of Cleo's insight—like asking for the wisdom of Solomon. She smiled. Cleo had to be the smartest person she knew.

"Okay, it's got to be in the car." Cleo jingled her keys and headed for the door.

"So what is this special movie that we have to watch?"

"It's a romantic suspense, about a small town, something about a mystery. . .there's a guy and a girl. . . Oh, what is the name of the thing?"

"Your favorite, huh?" Bethany threw a small handful of popcorn at the person she'd just decided was so wise.

"I know the actress in it. She was very popular at one time. But she died in a car accident while some photo hound was chasing her. Dee Bellamy." Cleo disappeared out the door to find the video.

Bethany sat in stunned silence, tears threatening to spill down her cheeks. She would force herself to pull together before Cleo returned. She had to.

eight

"You have to try this calamari," Chez said as he shoved another piece in his mouth.

Bethany laughed. "Go easy on that. You don't want to lose it when I beat you in my go-cart. Squid doesn't taste as good coming up as it does going down."

"No way can you beat the "King of Speed" himself. I live in California, you know."

Using her fork for emphasis, she stabbed the air. "I learned how to drive on the West Coast, so you've got nothing on me, buster!" She used the same fork as a bayonet, savagely spearing a piece of her grilled steak. Then she squeezed the seasoned meat between her teeth.

"So," Chez said, "tell me more about the play in the fall. I'm fascinated with Shakespeare."

Funny, he didn't seem like the bard type. "*As You Like It* is one of his most brilliant comedies, in my opinion. It's about subterfuge and people pretending to be what they aren't."

He colored slightly and cleared his throat. "Doesn't sound very funny to me."

She watched him fan himself slightly with his napkin and wondered if the humidity was getting to him. "It's the twist that's comical. The heroine pretends to be a man to protect herself from evil in the forest. Then, suddenly the one she has feelings for shows up, but she continues to pretend so she can find out what his true feelings are. It's a game."

"And you'll be playing the pretender."

"If I get the part. I've done this play in high school and professionally."

"I applaud your humility. What I hear, you're a shoo-in no matter what play they choose to do."

She felt herself blush. "You must have been talking to Cleo, my best friend. She would host my fan club if I had one. So far, she's it."

"Actually, if you're talking about the short redheaded chick, she doesn't seem to like me very much."

She reached over and placed her hand on his. "I'm sorry. She's very protective of me, as I would be of her. I'll talk to her if she makes you uncomfortable."

His smile showed perfect white teeth. "Naw. As long as she doesn't turn you against me, I'll be okay." He flipped his hand over offering her his palm, and she pulled away quickly.

Those eyes. How can they be ice blue and yet smolder at the same time? She pulled at the neck of her blouse. "It's stuffy in here. Are you about through?"

❧

Brick watched Bethany and the lizard as they entered The Track, her favorite amusement park. Phase Two had worked better than he'd hoped. He watched with satisfaction as they both recognized the Gulfarium employees and members of the filming crew milling about. Vet techs, snack bar employees, and aquarists careened crazily around an oval track, bumping into grips, gaffers, and lighting engineers. Chez's mouth had gone slack, and his eyes bugged like a carp. Bethany smiled broadly, obviously enjoying the surprise.

A cameraman flew past them but then stopped short. Turning, he grabbed Chez's hand and shook it. "Thanks, boss! This was a great idea. We needed to unwind after the grueling schedule you've had us on. You're the greatest!"

Chez stammered. "I—uh—I. . ."

Brick walked up to them and slapped him on the back. "Don't be modest, Chez-*Bud*." He turned to Bethany. "This guy booked the whole park just for us." With a light, *affectionate* slap to Chez's cheek, he said, "You'd better do something about the media, though. They're starting to gather. It'll be a circus soon if you don't gain control now." He motioned with his eyes to the newspaper and television news vans entering the parking lot. Two more slaps and he finished with "Good luck, *buddy*." He took Bethany's elbow and said, "It'll take him awhile to get things in order. Why don't we ride the go-carts until he can join us?"

Before Brick could pull Bethany away, she reached over and squeezed Chez's hand. "Thank you for the wonderful surprise." Brick's guts wrenched inside of him, but he knew he had to play it cool. It was all going as planned, and he couldn't let his jealousy ruin it for him.

As they walked away, he heard Chez call after them, perhaps a bit weakly, "Yeah, well. . .I'll catch up with you guys in a moment."

Brick hoped it would be a long moment. With the park open on all sides, Chez was faced with a security nightmare. *Heh-heh.*

They approached the go-carts, and Brick whispered, "Hey, Bethy, remember driver's ed?"

Her tinkling giggle nearly took his breath away. "You had poor Mr. Ludlow clinging to the dashboard. I think he left fingernail marks."

"What about you? You had the man vowing never to teach a woman driver again."

"Didn't he retire that year?" She had reached a red car and slung herself inside.

"Yeah, I wonder what he's doing now."

"I heard he became a shark trainer." Before he realized she was kidding, she hit the gas and took off. He hopped into a blue mini and followed in hot pursuit.

&

After the go-carts, Bethany decided a snow cone would hit the spot. While Ricky stood in line, Cleo arrived. She looked around. "Where's Chez? Aren't you supposed to be with him?"

Bethany shrugged. She realized she hadn't even missed him. "Didn't you see the media frenzy in the parking lot? Chez is in the middle of it, trying to keep his actors safe. He'll join us as soon as he can get away." She looked over at Ricky by the snow cone cart, and a niggling thought crept into her brain. Did she truly hope that Chez would be tied up all night? A feeling of guilt started chinking away at her conscience.

Ricky presented her snow cone and greeted Cleo.

"Cleo," Bethany said, "I'd like you to meet Rick—er—Brick Connor."

Ricky reached out his hand. "It's Brick legally, but I'm Ricky to my family and close friends." He winked at Bethany, and she squeezed her snow cone, almost popping off the rounded top.

Cleo held out her hand. "I'm Cleo, the annoying best friend, a mere subplot character."

Ricky's hearty laugh thundered, and Bethany almost felt jealous that it had been Cleo who'd elicited such a response and not herself. *Chink, chink.* More guilt.

"You're never a mere subplot character," Ricky said. "See that fella over there?" He pointed to Vince Galloway, who was cheering on a child as she somersaulted on the trampoline. "He started out as a subplot character in the first *Danger* movie. We had such a great response that he's now Agent Danger's main nemesis. Everyone loves to hate Shark Finlay." He leaned over to whisper in confidence. "And in real life, he's *my* annoying best friend." He held up his paper cone, which was already beginning to drip. "Would you like something? My treat."

"No thanks, I'm good."

He crunched off a big bite from the top of the ice cone, slurping with satisfaction. "Bethany and I were headed for the bumper boats. You game?"

Cleo looked at Bethany. *Do you want me to come?* she silently communicated. Bethany couldn't think of anything more pleasant than an evening with the love of her past and her best friend, annoying though she may be. Funny, Chez didn't figure into the equation. *Chink.*

੨ð

The threesome became four when Brick invited Vince along for minigolf. Chez was still busy with the reporters, probably giving an interview to some pretty young thing, no doubt lining up his conquests. Brick shuddered. He remembered when he had been that slimy. Thankfully, he grew out of it. If only Chez would. He'd get a lot further in his career if he'd lay off the drinking and carousing.

Cleo and Vince chose their colored golf balls and moved to the side of the little building to pick up their clubs. As Bethany stepped up to the rack of balls with all the different options, Brick couldn't resist playing an old childhood game. "Wait. Let me guess. Which one would Bethy pick today?" He looked at what she was wearing. A pink T-shirt with blue shorts. On the left leg was a pink embroidered flower. "Pink for the lady."

Bethany colored prettily, her blush complementing her shirt. "Did I always choose according to how I dressed?"

"Always." He couldn't tear his eyes from her. The years scattered and blew away like dead leaves, and they were Ricky and Bethy again. It was all he could do not to lean down and kiss those perfect pink lips.

"Hey, you two joining us, or what?"

"Yeah, we can't be a foursome without you."

The two annoying best friends. Yes, he was in high school again, and Bethy was his girl.

"Blue." Bethy tapped his arm.

"What?"

"Blue for you." He came out of his dream, reluctantly.

"How do you know? I never chose according to what I wore."

"Because, you always picked blue. It's your favorite color." She sashayed away from him, obviously satisfied to have matched him in the game.

"Oh, yeah." His voice cracked. *No way, Chez. No way are you going to have any more to do with this woman.*

&

They had made it to the sixteenth hole. Bethany felt like a kid again. And why not, when she was practically reliving her childhood. She'd been to The Track dozens of times. Sometimes with a group from church. Sometimes with Cleo. But never with Ricky O'Connell. She knew she would cherish this new memory and never think of this place again without seeing him by her side. Teasing her as she flubbed the ball, or accidentally hitting it over the barrier... She would always see the intensity of his concentration as he strove to make a hole in one. How she wished this night could continue. But, of course, that would be impossible.

Suddenly it was over. Chez jogged up to them, putter in hand.

"Man, it's a jungle out there. But I think I got everything under control." He took Bethany's hand and said, "I'm sorry it took me so long. Ended up doing an impromptu interview."

"It's fine. I'm sorry you've missed half the evening."

"You kidding? Now the real fun begins, love."

A sudden movement caught her eye, and Bethany realized Vince had grabbed Ricky's right arm. Something was going on between those two.

"I told the reporters that both of you would give an interview," Chez said. "They were excited that you were such good friends in real life. It'll give them a thrill to see enemies on the screen buddying up. They're waiting for you." When neither man budged, he prompted, "If you don't go now, they'll come looking for you. At least they're corralled in the parking lot."

Ricky looked into Bethany's eyes, and she read regret. It thrilled her to think he'd rather stay with her.

When he spoke, his words belied what she'd just sensed from him. "Oh well, the life of an actor. We're on twenty-four seven. It's been fun, girls."

"So." Chez draped his arm over Bethany's shoulders and looked from her to Cleo. "Let's finish this course and move on to the other one. I hear it's harder."

nine

"CLEO BABY!"

Bethany's best friend whipped her head around to find the voice calling her.

"Ed?"

The large man sprinted over outdoor carpet and around fake jungle creatures. Cleo dropped her club and ran to him, jumping into his outstretched arms. "What are you doing back so soon? I wasn't expecting you for two days."

"I never question the Air Force. If they want to send me home, I'm not going to ask why. Apparently there was a space available, and they offered it to me." The munitions expert dwarfed his pixie wife, yet they were a matched set. He looked over his wife's head and said, "Hi, Bethany."

"Hi, Ed. Welcome home."

Cleo tilted her strawberry curls and asked, "How did you know I was here?"

"Are you kidding? It's all over the news. I got home to an empty house and turned on the TV. When they said the filming crew and the Gulfarium had taken over this place, I knew I'd find you here. You'd never miss excitement like this."

She held up her putter. "We're about to start another game. Do you want to join us?"

Ed's smoldering gaze spoke volumes. Cleo looked at Bethany and said, "Bye!"

"Boy, I know where I rank now." Bethany received a fierce hug from her best friend. "Go, be with your husband."

Cleo needed little encouragement.

When they were gone, Chez spoke with a bad imitation of Humphrey Bogart. "Just you and me, kid. Let's blow this Popsicle stand."

"I suppose things will wind down soon, and I do have work tomorrow." She would rather have stayed, but without Cleo or Ricky, she found her energy waning.

As they walked to the parking lot, Chez said, "Actually, I saw that the boardwalk had a nice nightspot. Maybe we could do some dancing."

"I'm not much of a nightspot type of gal."

"Well," he said, scratching his head, "we have to go back there to get your car anyway. How about coffee at the restaurant?"

He is persistent. Maybe she should cap off the evening with something to eat. What harm could there be in that? "Sure. They have outside tables so we can continue to enjoy this beautiful night."

She found herself looking around for Ricky and Vince. If she caught them in time, she'd invite them along. Unfortunately, the newspeople were packing up their vans, the interview apparently over. She had no idea where the two may have gone.

When they reached his car, Chez held the door open for her. "The boardwalk it is then. I promise I won't keep you out much later. I just haven't been able to spend as much time with you as I would have liked."

Bethany decided this would be a perfect time to get rid of the guilt she'd been feeling about not missing Chez.

❧

Brick headed back to the minigolf course. Bethany and Chez were nowhere to be found. He'd seen Cleo leave with someone, which meant Bethany was alone with the leech. If he hadn't allowed the photo op with Vince in the bumper cars, he may have caught them in time.

He went back toward the parking lot. Chez's car was gone. A man from the camera crew approached him from the direction of the lot. After a brief greeting, Brick asked, "Hey, you didn't happen to see Chez out there, did you?"

"Yeah, I saw him and that blond dolphin cutie getting into the car I parked next to. I heard them say something about the boardwalk; they're going there for coffee. But I'll bet Chez has dessert on his mind." He gave an evil wink, placed his hands in his pockets, and sauntered into the amusement park, whistling.

☙

Chez pulled a chair out for Bethany. When the waitress arrived to take their order, they both decided neither was hungry enough for a snack. Chez ordered coffee, and Bethany ordered hot tea. "Oh." Chez caught the waitress before she walked away. "Make that to go."

"Why?" A rock suddenly dropped into the pit of Bethany's stomach.

"I thought maybe we could take our drinks and walk the beach."

Bethany looked where he indicated. It was well lit, and there were still a few die-hard tourists milling about. "If we don't go far. Like I said, I have to work tomorrow."

"Absolutely." He smiled, but his eyes didn't seem as friendly as the rest of his face.

Once on the beach, Bethany suddenly felt vulnerable. She didn't know if it was the black haze over the Gulf, or the wide expanse of beach beyond the pools of light illuminating the area from floodlights on the building. A breeze had kicked up, and she shivered, wishing she had brought her sweater.

"Are you cold?" Chez slipped his arm around her shoulder and rubbed her skin. "Drink your tea. That should warm you up."

He started walking out of the safety of the lights, where the beach was deserted. She stopped. "Chez, I don't feel comfortable going any farther."

He peered into the darkness. "Just to that bit of wood there. I want to see if it's from a shipwreck." When she hesitated, he said, "Don't worry; I'm here."

She allowed him to pull her along, wanting with all her heart to prove Cleo wrong.

Chez kicked the wood. "Aw, can't tell what it is in this light." He turned to her and cupped her chin. "But you look beautiful.

Let's see what's on the other side of that bush."

Bethany pulled away, but he clamped down on her hand. A movement near the bush caught her eye. Bethany's nerves were already about to snap, but seeing a broad figure standing in the shadows caused a scream to form in her chest. *Does he have an accomplice? I can't fight two of them!*

Just then, Vince Galloway walked into the moonlight.

"Vince!" Chez bellowed. "What are you doing lurking in the dark? Studying for a new role?"

"I came here same as you." He indicated the Styrofoam cups in their hands. "Do you mind if I tag along? I miss my family and don't feel like sitting in my empty hotel room."

"Please, join us," Bethany said, grateful to Vince for his intervention. She silently lifted a prayer of thanksgiving. Had Chez lured her out there for a reason? Or was it just her imagination? "That is, if Chez doesn't mind." It wouldn't matter if he did. She was not going to be alone with him.

She received a look from Chez that frightened her. Apparently he did mind. But then, as a chameleon changing its color to suit its environment, Chez smiled and said too politely, "You know, you've been telling me all evening you needed to get home. Maybe we should call it a night."

They walked back to the parking lot, with Vince bringing up the rear, like a watchful guardian.

"Vince, do you mind?" Chez flung over his shoulder. "I'd like to say a proper good night to my date."

"Oh, sorry. My car is over there. See you tomorrow, Bethany."

When they reached her car, she opened her door. Chez caressed her shoulders as he turned her to face him. "I had a good time tonight, despite the fiasco with the reporters."

As he spoke, he drew closer to her. The roof of her car bit into her shoulder blade.

Whoop! Whoop! Scree! Scree! Whoop! Whoop!

Chez jumped back as if electrocuted. Vince's car seemed to be having a conniption fit. The horn blared, and the lights flashed. With a *blip-blip*, it stopped.

"Sorry, it's a rental," Vince called out. "Not used to it, I guess. Hit the alarm button by mistake."

Bethany took the opportunity to slip into her car. She shut the door and rolled down the window only enough to talk. When Chez turned back toward her, she could see his intense disappointment.

"Thank you for the surprise. It was so thoughtful of you to include everyone in our night of fun. I'll see you tomorrow."

She backed out of the space and waved at Vince as she drove by. In her rearview mirror, she witnessed Chez kicking the pavement in frustration.

❧

Brick watched from his own car, several rows away. After throwing a little hissy fit, Chez threw himself into his car and whipped out of the parking lot. Brick could imagine him sulking.

As Vince drove toward the exit, Brick saw a thick, stubby thumb raised in triumph from the driver-side window. He responded in kind, very pleased with himself that the plan had gone so well. Not only had he gotten the chance to be with Bethany, but because of his ex-friend's predictable nature, he hoped he had orchestrated Chez's fall. Surely she must have seen the lizard's true colors.

He followed him back to the hotel.

ten

Bethany knew about the benefit to help buy resources for the Stranded Fund, a charity set up to help animals that had beached themselves. She was shocked to find out, by reading a poster in the gift shop, that Galaxy Productions had agreed to be a part of it.

" 'Brick Connor and Vince Galloway will be available for autographs and pictures'," she read aloud to Cleo. "They've set it for the night after the film crew leaves."

"I know; I taped that up there." Cleo zipped and locked her cash bag, tucked it under her arm, then reached for her purse. "Too bad I'm going to miss it."

"You can't leave and miss the glitz and glamour."

Cleo locked the door for the final time before her vacation as she said, "Sorry, but I've had these plane tickets for weeks. I guess I'll have to create my own glitz and glamour with the man I love in his parents' mountain lodge. I understand we'll have the guest cabin out back."

"That sounds like more fun than a stuffy benefit. Can I come?"

"Only if you board with the family." Cleo gave a mischievous wink.

Bethany would miss her. But another void in her heart took precedence. Production would wrap up this week, and things would go back to normal. *Normal.* That word sounded so— *normal.* Mundane. Boring. Brickless. *Whoa! Where did that come from?* The man whom she told to stay out of her life would actually be leaving it. How did she feel about that?

Every time she tried to convince herself that she was happy her life would get back to—*normal,* she would see herself laughing with Ricky, whipping around a track in a little metal car, splashing him with her bumper boat. She'd had fun last night. Could she let him fade from her life again? What choice did she have? He belonged to the world now. An emptiness engulfed her that she hadn't felt in ten years.

And what about Chez? She knew the answer to that one. Chez had become someone else: the person Cleo saw—the person Ricky warned her about. She felt God had opened her eyes last night, probably due to her friend's prayers.

She decided to avoid Chez throughout the week. But when he sought her out the last evening of shooting, she agreed to talk to him. He probably only wanted to say good-bye. They walked to the bench overlooking the Gulf. A fog over the water filtered the sun as it tried to burn through, causing an eerie, yellowish glow.

The crew milled about the Shark Moat, which was nearby, so she wouldn't be alone with Chez. She wrapped her arms around herself and faced away from him.

"I just wanted to tell you," he said as he started to caress her shoulder, "that I enjoyed our brief time together. How about the benefit tomorrow? Would you like to pick me up? I've already turned in my rental."

"Um, Chez." She wiggled away from his touch. "I don't know if I'm going." She didn't know why she hadn't thought that he might ask her to the benefit.

"That's okay. We could ditch the whole thing and pick up where we left off at the beach."

"I don't think so. It's best we say our good-byes."

"I never say good-bye." His hand slipped around hers, and he began to stroke her palm.

She whipped her hand away and turned to face him. *Oh no, you don't, buster. I'm on to you.*

"We'll see each other again," he continued. "Maybe when this movie is done, I'll come back. Then we'll have more time to get to know each other."

When he squeezed her upper arms, she placed her hands on his chest. Apparently he didn't care who witnessed this scene. She tried to push him away, but he had latched onto her shoulders, drawing her closer, obviously for a kiss.

"Stop!" In what seemed like phenomenal strength, she pushed him so hard he flew into the air. However, it had been Ricky who grabbed the smaller man by the shoulders and yanked him away from her.

"What the lady is trying to tell you is that it's over."

Ricky glared down at Chez on the ground. She had never seen him that angry, not even in his movies.

Chez blinked and shook his head as if stunned to find himself on the concrete looking up. "That's the last time, Connor," he snarled through gritted teeth. "You can't bully your way out of this one."

"You going to use your mouth to fight, as usual?"

Chez let out a war cry and took the actor head-on. Bethany held in a scream as the two men wrestled. Alarmed, she watched Ricky get a left handhold on the front of Chez's shirt and prepare to swing with his right. She grabbed his fist. "Stop! He's no match for you. And not worth going to jail over."

A muscle rippled in his jaw. After several seconds, he grabbed the director's clothing with both fists and flung him toward the beach, where he landed in the soft, white sand. While Chez sputtered and spit granules out of his mouth, Ricky thrust a pointed finger at him. "Leave her alone. She tried to be subtle, but you're too thick to see she was trying to get rid of you."

Chez stood up, wiped sand off his face, and hopped back over the railing. "You're going to be sorry you did that, Connor," he said as he retreated back to the set.

Ricky turned toward Bethany, who still stood with her mouth agape. His velvet voice caressed her. "Are you okay?"

Bile rose in her throat like mercury in a hot thermometer, the acid taste a reminder of how vulnerable she had been. How many girls had Chez gotten into the moonlight? How many against their will? She started to shiver, and her chin began to tremble. Ricky wrapped his arms around her. She buried her face into the lining of his leather jacket and dug her fingernails into the pliable softness of the lapel. Her tears came hot and plentiful, but they weren't only because of Chez. The familiar feel of her first love's arms triggered memories. . .his fingers caressing her hair. . .the gentle voice that once spoke tender words of love. . . .

Different hands on her shoulders pulled her away from where she belonged. *No*, she wanted to scream. *I'm not done savoring this moment*. . .the smell of leather mingled with spicy cologne. . .the broad chest and muscled arms created to hold her exclusively. Her father pulled his only child from Ricky's arms and curled her into his own.

"What happened here?"

Only then did she realize they had drawn an audience. Forty concerned faces watched as her father led her away to his office.

As she looked back, a vision of the boy who had adored her blurred into the man she could never have, and she longed to be sixteen again.

❧

Brick punched Bethany's phone number while in his hotel room. He'd left the set early, not willing to be near Chez anymore. What shots were left could be handled by his double. He desperately wanted to talk to her—no—he wanted to hold her again. He could thank Chez for that incredible moment. Bethy nuzzled to his chest, her soft hair tickling his lips. The smell of coconut-scented lotion drifting into his senses, making him long to dip into her slender neck for more.

He counted three rattling rings through the receiver before he heard a male voice. "Hello?"

"Glenn, it's Brick. How's Bethany? May I talk to her?"

"She'll be fine. Just a minute."

The voices were muffled, as if Glenn had covered the mouthpiece. It sounded like they were arguing, but after a long moment, Bethany came on the phone.

"Hello, Ricky."

He swallowed hard. *Get a grip; you're not a teenager anymore.*

"Hi, how are you doing?"

An unsteady sigh made his heart break. "How should I be? I feel like a fool. You tried to warn me, but I wouldn't listen. Even Cleo could see what kind of person he was."

"Don't be too hard on yourself. Chez makes a career of deceiving women. I should have stopped him before he had a chance to do it to you."

"Well, fortunately the only thing hurt was my pride. Thank you for intervening tonight."

"My pleasure." He genuinely meant that.

"I guess this is good-bye, then."

His heart constricted. "Won't I see you at the benefit tomorrow?"

"I'm not going. I'm not in the party mood."

"But it's for your animals. How would it look for the Gulfarium's most valued asset to be absent from her own party?"

She chuckled, but there was little mirth in the sound. "I'm hardly an asset, more of a liability, actually. Listen, let's just end it here. It's been great seeing you again. Good luck with your career."

Was she really talking to him as if he were a mere acquaintance from the past? *Oh no, you don't, Bethy dear. I have a plan.* "Uh, yeah, and you with yours. Put your father on, okay? In case things get crazy tomorrow, I'd like to say my good-byes tonight."

When Glenn came back on the phone, Brick said, "Listen, could you do me a favor?"

❧

"That one." Glenn pointed to the second dress Bethany held up. That was her favorite, too, but for some reason, her mind fogged over every time she thought about the benefit. Cleo would normally be helping her make this important decision, but she had already left for Colorado.

"Okay, the pink dress." She tossed the off-the-shoulder number on her bed. "Now, how about shoes?"

"Don't make me sorry I talked you into this, daughter," Glenn groaned.

"Oh, all right. I only have a couple of pairs of shoes that would work anyway."

Her father, who had been sitting at her vanity, stood and walked toward the door. He looked at his watch. "I'm going to eat some lunch, then head over there to help set up. I want to be sure they put the band in the right place."

Bethany was so proud of her dad. He'd been in the swing band for years, and now he not only played lead trumpet but directed, as well. Whenever she'd been at other functions with him, she loved to watch the audience, many of them middle-aged women, swaying to the music and batting their eyelashes at him as if he were Glenn Miller himself.

He continued. "I'll be back to get you in plenty of time. But I'm taking my tux just in case I can't get away."

Bethany picked up the pink dress and looked in her full-length mirror, holding the hanger under her chin and swishing the netted fabric to test the movement. "If that happens, I can drive myself."

"No, I need a date. We can't have the most eligible bachelor in northwest Florida going stag, now can we?" He walked back into the room and kissed her hair. "You just better be ready. None of that *making the date wait* stuff. I'm an old man and don't have time for such foolishness." He winked as he left the room.

Later that evening, while putting the finishing touches to her makeup, she heard the doorbell ring. She looked at her watch, wondering where her father was. Then a thought hit her. "That scamp!" she said to her cat, which was pawing at a round perfume bottle on the vanity. "He's pretending to be my date by picking me up at the door."

She descended the stairs, smoothing her dress and fluffing her hair. With her most gracious smile in place, she grabbed the knob and flung open the door for her date.

"You're right on ti—"

Brick Connor, multimillion-dollar box office star, stood on her doorstep in full tux and holding a corsage.

eleven

"Your father regrets his absence and has asked me to take his place. I hope that's suitable for you."

Her mouth lay open with the last word she tried to utter still stuck in her throat. She dumbly nodded her head and allowed him to pin the delicate flowers to her dress. A slight breeze caused his spicy cologne to intermingle with the scent of the tiny pink roses, and the combination muddled her thinking.

Why was she acting so silly? After all, wasn't this Ricky, her childhood friend? She took in the tailored tux, the silk shirt, the imported shoes. His dark hair and mustache, his brown contact-tinted eyes—the whole image was a direct negative of the boy she once loved. Ricky had been a golden child, light hair that only grew lighter in the sun, green eyes that reflected the nature around him. However, she reacted to this man in a perfectly normal way. She became Cinderella, and he was the prince of the silver screen.

She still hadn't said a word when her date lowered himself into the BMW and chuckled. "This kinda reminds me of prom." The compact hummed to life at the driver's touch, and music began to flow from the CD player.

Smooth jazz filled the small compartment, helping to untie Bethany's tongue and her tangled emotions. She wondered about her father but, knowing how much he liked Ricky, sensed he had something to do with this *change of plans*.

She narrowed her eyes and cast a sideward glance at the stranger by her side. "Did you two plan this?" When he feigned confusion, she clarified. "You and my dad."

"I confess. I bribed him." Her skepticism must have been evident because he quickly added, "Okay. I asked him to let me do this. I needed a time to be alone with you, to talk."

"We talked the other night."

"While screaming around a go-cart track? Come on, Bethy. While that was all great fun, we never had a chance to clear the air between us."

"What's to clear? I think I clarified everything that first night. We've both moved on. I'm not the same person, and obviously, neither are you."

He began tapping the steering wheel in time to the music. She had to hide a grin. Maybe he hadn't changed so much. He still fidgeted when he was nervous.

"Look," he said as they turned onto the highway, "I'm not suggesting we get back together." Bethany felt her heart thud. Was that what she had wanted all along?

"Neither am I." Her sullen reflection in the passenger-side window suggested otherwise.

"I would just like to know what happened and renew at least a friendship. Is that too much to ask?"

She turned toward him, taking in his now-mature profile. The baby fat was gone, the freckles had faded away, his neck fit snugly into his collar, and those shoulders. . .

His mouth was moving; she'd better start to pay attention. ". . .thought someday you'd join me."

"What?"

"We were quite the team in high school. In fact, you were phenomenal. I only stuck with it to be with you. You were a much better actor than me."

"That's not true. How could you have gotten this far if you weren't good?"

"I didn't say I wasn't good; I said you were better. I've gotten this far with an exceptional manager and superb advice. I thought someday we'd be a team, like Taylor and Burton. . . ."

"Divorced, several times."

"Tracy and Hepburn."

"Living in sin."

"Rooney and Garland."

"Just good friends."

He grabbed the gearshift and popped it into fifth. "You're not making this easy."

She felt her ears buzz with adrenaline. "Why should I make it easy? You abandoned me."

He whipped his head to look at her. "You're the one who left. How can you say I abandoned you?"

"You stopped writing." She began to pick at her newly polished nails.

"You did, too."

She drew in a shaky breath. Someone had to be the mature one; it might as well be her. "I guess it's as I said before. We just outgrew each other. It happens."

&

It happens.

Brick chewed the inside of his cheek. Could she actually be this nonchalant about their relationship? He knew beyond any shadow of a doubt, that if she had stayed in California, they would have married.

"Even if you hadn't moved and we had stayed together, it still wouldn't be the same as it was. People grow up, Bethany. It doesn't have to end simply because we're older."

"It's not because we're older, Ricky. It's because we're different. There was a time we were so in tune we could finish each other's thoughts."

"Because we were together so much. That's the only thing I can be grateful to my father for." The familiar surge of hatred boiled deep under the surface, and he rubbed at the scar on his chin.

Bethany patted his arm. "I know. You spent more time at my house than your own, just to avoid him."

She removed her hand too quickly. He wanted to reach with his left, and hold it against his sleeve, like a captured butterfly. But the elusive fingers fluttered away, leaving the skin under his jacket tingling, longing for another touch.

"If it hadn't been for that," he agreed, "I wouldn't have grown so close to you, or your family."

As they sat in silence, a saxophone drawled a bittersweet tune, somehow musically describing the mood.

᲼

Music erupted from Ricky's breast pocket. Bethany frowned as he pulled out a cell phone. "Are you in position?" He glanced around, apparently looking for street signs. "We're almost there." He turned down a dark road with a sign pointing to the beach.

"What's going on?" Surely he wasn't going to try to kidnap her so they could spend time together. That was absurd.

"Your dad told me how you felt about people seeing us together. He's going to meet us and take you the rest of the way. This is going to be a media event tonight, and if you're seen arriving with me, they'll be all over you."

Touched by his thoughtfulness, she realized he had all the power. If he wanted to parade her before the cameras, he certainly could. She remembered back a mere twenty-four hours, when Chez had gone sailing over the rail. Brick Connor was not a man to provoke. And yet his gentleness defined his character.

As a result of this new revelation, she couldn't have kept her next words from spilling out of her mouth if she had jammed something between her teeth. "I hope that doesn't mean we have to avoid each other at the party."

He looked at her and swerved a little but regained control of the car quickly. "Nothing would keep us apart tonight."

They met her father at a parking area near a deserted beach where Bethany traded cars. Ricky gave them a few minutes' head start, and they arrived at the hotel moments before him.

Glenn got out of the car, walked to the passenger side, and offered his hand to Bethany. She sat there, arms folded, staring forward.

"Come on, honey," he pleaded.

The valet stood patiently waiting with a smirk on his face. "Trouble with the little woman, sir?"

Bethany stifled a giggle. She heard her dad say, "The little woman is my daughter," as he bent down, his face scowling at her from the open door, and finished the sentence, "and she's being a brat."

Bethany gracefully turned and stepped out of the car. She was gratified by an appreciative look from the valet. Glenn scowled when he handed him the keys, and the boy quickly said, "Yes, sir."

Bethany refused Glenn's outstretched hand. "I'm not speaking to you."

"Okay, I'm sorry I deceived you. But he's a very persuasive man."

They moved toward the glass doors of the hotel. A gold rope had been placed to form an alley to the ballroom, and on either side were anxious faces looking for their favorite star. Bethany heard whispering, and it was clear they were trying to decide if she and her escort were famous. Then she heard someone over the din. "Oh, those are just the fish people."

That did it. She couldn't keep up her pretend anger any longer. With a chuckle, she turned toward her father. "You shouldn't have conspired with him, you know."

"I know, but he's like a son to me. What could I do?"

"Well, since I'm like a daughter to you, you should have protected me."

She tucked her hands into the crook of his arm and leaned close. "But thank you. It felt good to talk to him without an audience eavesdropping." She placed a perfectly formed *mauvelous*-colored lip print on his cheek and then wiped it off with her thumb.

As they moved into the ballroom and were escorted to the head table, both were struck by the glamour of it all. Bethany turned to her father and whispered, "I don't think we're in Kansas anymore, Toto." She had been in this ballroom for a wedding reception before, but then it never looked like something out of a Hollywood movie. Candles flickered in real crystal vases, causing the glow on the walls and ceiling to dance. Glitter sparkled on tables, on plants, and on the floor. There were two ice sculptures spouting a sparkling beverage.

One was a dolphin, in leap mode. The other was a kangaroo, to represent the movie, *Danger Down Under.*

"How delightfully decadent," Bethany said as her father pulled the chair out for her.

Even so, all of that paled when compared to the man entering the room. Brick Connor made his grand appearance with the self-assuredness of Cary Grant, the panache of Fred Astaire, and the mystique of Sean Connery.

Vince Galloway entered with Ricky, but it was obvious whom the crowd was there to see. Cameras clicked wildly as local and Hollywood reporters clamored for a comment. The two men moved to a microphone. After the commotion died down, Ricky said, "I, along with Vince Galloway and Galaxy Productions, would like to thank the fine people of Fort Walton Beach for their cooperation in the making of the film, *Danger Down Under.*" This was met with wild applause and whistles. He went on to thank every organization that offered its support and every official involved.

"And now, I'd like to introduce the man responsible for this event."

Simon Kimball came forward. A large screen had been set up, and he began narrating a computer presentation depicting a dolphin rescue that had happened within the last year. When the presentation was over, he received a standing ovation.

As Bethany sat back down, she wondered briefly who would fill the empty chairs around her table. She assumed Simon would take one. Then she smelled that cologne. The lightest touch of his fingers on her shoulders caused her whole body to react, and she grabbed her napkin to still her trembling hands. The voice behind her betrayed his nearness, and she heard a whispered, "How fortunate that we're seated together."

Glenn, on her right, introduced everyone as the large round table began to fill. This included Vince Galloway, Simon and his wife, the mayor and her husband, as well as Cassie, their teenage daughter, apparently a huge Brick Connor fan. Bethany thought the child would die of pent-up excitement.

She had obviously been taught how to behave at functions, but if she sparkled any more, there would be no need for the glitter that adorned the room.

Bethany commented on the empty chair next to Cassie. All eyes turned to the vacant chair, and Ricky answered. "That was supposed to be for Chad Cheswick, the assistant director for this location shoot." He reached for his water and sipped before saying, "He was called away—rather unexpectedly last night." Bethany hid a smile as he whispered behind the goblet, "Or rather *sent* away."

The meal started with a creamy broccoli cheese soup with bits of potato, followed by a crunchy cabbage salad with sesame seeds and almonds. The entrée, a scrumptious apricot-glazed chicken garnished with seedless grapes, was accompanied by a side dish of ginger-fried rice. The entire meal ended with almond praline cheesecake.

While coffee was served, Glenn excused himself. "I'm going to try to work after eating all this food. Forgive me if my trumpet sounds flat. My stomach muscles may not be able to sustain the notes."

The waiter came to Bethany, and she refused coffee but asked for herbal tea. Ricky had been in a conversation with the mayor and hadn't heard her request. So when he also asked for herbal tea, something within her struck a chord. Could there still be hope for the two of them? Perhaps she should pursue what they had in common rather than dwell on their differences.

However, there was one huge difference. Ricky no longer lived for the Lord.

Vince rose, also excusing himself, and motioned for Ricky to follow.

Ricky touched his napkin to the corners of his mouth. "Gentlemen. Ladies." He looked at Bethany, and she felt a blush on her cheeks. "Forgive me, but there is already a line forming at the autograph table."

The swing band began with a crashing beat, and soon the dance floor was filled with jitterbugs.

twelve

Bethany leaned her elbows on the linen tablecloth and cupped her chin as she looked around the ballroom. Couples everywhere. She longed for Cleo's chatty presence. But even if her friend hadn't deserted her to go to Colorado, Ed would be with her. Just another couple to envy.

Bethany felt like a small fish in a very big sea.

After an hour, the musicians had stopped playing, taking a much-needed break, so she decided to search out her father. At least if she were standing next to a man, she'd feel like a couple, even if she did have genetic ties to him.

When she couldn't find him inside the ballroom, she went out to the patio that looked over the Gulf. The muggy breeze did little to cool her cheeks as she stepped outside.

She scanned the area. Several people had decided to get some fresh air, but in the corner, behind the potted ficus tree, was her father. He stood talking to someone hidden from view. Probably another member of the band. She'd go over and say hi.

When she approached, however, she witnessed an arm and a hand with French manicured nails wrap around his waist. *Who is this?*

Should she approach them? Would she be intruding? She felt an unexpected sharp pain. She'd seen her father with women before but knew he'd never felt serious toward any of them. His body language with this one suggested otherwise.

While she stood in the middle of the patio, pondering her decision, a voice from behind made her jump. "A lady shouldn't be standing all alone."

She turned to see Ricky's grin, and then she relaxed. "You startled me."

"You were deep in thought. Is everything okay?" He handed

her a glass of sparkling ginger ale.

"Thank you. I need this." She took a sip.

"Let's sit down over here on this bench." She looked around for someone to spring from the bushes with a camera. He must have sensed her hesitation. "Relax. I've been mingling with everyone; you're next in line. Now tell me what's bothering you."

She glanced over by the tree, but the couple—yes, it looked as though her father had become a *couple*—was gone.

❧

Bethany set her drink down and began to fiddle with her fingers. Brick dared to reach over and cup them with his hand. It pleased him when she didn't pull away.

"I guess I'm tired." She shrugged her slender shoulders. "It's been a long evening."

"Yeah. It's exhausting to have to smile and carry on a conversation with people you don't know." He reluctantly released her hands.

She looked at him, her lovely mouth at an angle. "How do you do it? You work long hours, you give interviews; is there ever a time when you relax between movies?"

"I haven't had a real vacation in years. We've been making the *Danger* movies back-to-back." He sighed heavily. "I'll admit, I'm beginning to burn out."

"Maybe you should take a break after this project. Lounge on a beach somewhere. Go surfing. Do you still do that?"

He shook his head. "I haven't been surfing in years. I still have the board, though."

"You're kidding. As many times as you wiped out?"

He chuckled. "You wiped out a few times yourself, dudette. I remember when we were both on that board. . . ." She squirmed slightly, and he knew he'd overstepped the boundary. "Anyway, a vacation is just what I need. I'll arrange it when I get home."

She glanced around the patio and said, "Looks like everyone's gone inside now that the music has started up again."

His arm acted on its own volition, and he reached around her shoulders. She looked up at him, and in the tiny white lights entwined through a trellis nearby, he could see her emerald green eyes. "You know, your eyes are the color of the coast. You blend in beautifully with your surroundings here."

A light floral fragrance had replaced her tropical-scented suntan lotion. It invited him closer, closer, until their lips nearly touched.

"Ricky." She put her hand on his chest. "I need to go inside." She stood and walked away from him.

He scratched his head.

Well, that *never happened to Brick Connor before.*

❧

Please don't let me topple off these shoes. She could feel his eyes on her back, and her already-wobbly state threatened to buckle her ankles. *Don't let yourself fall for him again. You'll only get hurt.* But even as she thought those words, she knew it was too late.

Glenn announced they would play "Waltzing Matilda" for their final song in honor of *Danger Down Under.* Like Cinderella, Bethany believed she'd never see her prince again after she left the ball. She mingled while saying good-bye to the crew.

Vince swept her off her feet in a boisterous hug. "It was sure a pleasure meeting you, Bethany." He nodded toward Ricky who was deep in a conversation with Glenn. "I'll take good care of him. He told me he'd accepted the Lord years ago but has fallen away. He has a lot of questions, and I think he may be ready to hear the answers." He winked, and she knew in her spirit, as she had on the first day, that Vince Galloway was indeed an answer to her petitions on Ricky's behalf. "When this young man finds his way back, God and His angels will give you a big thumbs-up for all your prayers."

Bethany threw her arms around her new friend's thick neck. "Thank you, Vince," she rasped. The tears were so close; if she had said any more, she'd have embarrassed herself.

As he walked away, he said, "Remember me when you par the eighteenth hole next time."

"I will." She twirled, her version of the happy dance, and

walked toward the table where her father and Ricky were.

Glenn stood, kissed her on the cheek, and offered to meet her in the lobby. He had some final things to do with the band before he could go home.

"Have a seat." Ricky pulled out a chair for her.

"What were you two talking so seriously about?" She fluffed her dress as she sat.

"Guy stuff—you wouldn't be interested."

She never understood the relationship between the two men.

Ricky pulled out a pen and began writing on a napkin.

"Now what are you doing?" Bethany peeked over the left hand that anchored the napkin.

"I'm pretending that you asked for my autograph. We're being watched carefully. I have to make it look like you're just another fan." With a playful grin, he whispered, "Try to look awestruck. You know, totally blown away by my star status."

Bethany pulled off her part to perfection, making her moony eyes drip with admiration.

He chuckled. "I knew you were a better actor than me." He gave her the napkin and shook her hand, making a point to caress her wrist with his thumb before letting go. "Good-bye, Bethy. I'll miss you."

She tucked the napkin inside her purse. "Good-bye, Ricky." With a lump the size of an Oscar statuette lodged in her throat, she turned and ran. She even thought of losing her shoe so he would have to track her down to give it to her.

Bethany waited in the lobby, waving to people as they left. Finally her father walked through the doors. S*he* was with him.

The woman hanging on her father's arm wasn't slender, by any means, certainly not athletic enough to keep up with him. Her short dark hair framed a fiftyish face. He introduced her as Amanda Schnell, a Realtor he'd met the previous December at a Chamber of Commerce Christmas party.

Bethany shook her hand carefully, avoiding the long fingernails. *Schnell, huh? Doesn't that mean* fast *in German?*

"Amanda and I had a couple of dates at the beginning of the

year," Glenn interjected. "Then she went out of town, and we lost touch. I told you about her, didn't I?"

Bethany cleared her throat. He expected her to talk? "Yes, you probably did, but you go out with so many women, I can't keep track of them all." *There. That should put Ms. Fast-with-the-Fingernails in her place.* But when she caught the warning look from her father, she immediately felt remorseful.

"When I saw her here, of all places," Glenn continued, "I wanted to make sure she wouldn't slip away from me again." He placed his arm around Amanda's shoulders and gave her a little squeeze.

Amanda patted his hand. With regard to Bethany, she said, "As a long-standing member of the Chamber of Commerce, I received an invitation to this prodigious cause. Knowing your father was involved, I wanted to come and support him."

Bethany watched the two gaze into each other's eyes. She hadn't seen that look on her father's face since her mother was alive. "That's nice." She didn't mean to sound so cold. Or did she? "I'll go have the valet pull the car around." She turned to flee but then remembered her manners. She turned and said, "It was nice meeting you, Amanda."

When she reached the cool night air, the valet grinned at her. "Did you ditch your *dad*? I get off in a half hour."

Before Bethany could think of a snappy retort, she heard her father's voice behind her. "The blue Blazer."

"Yes, sir."

Glenn glared at the valet as he hurried off to find the car. "Smart-aleck kid." While they waited, he seemed to search Bethany's face. "You okay?"

Bethany folded her arms around herself and felt the first sting of what she knew would be a bucketful of tears if she chose to release them.

The SUV was brought around. When they were well on their way, Bethany couldn't voice what was in her heart—that she may never see Ricky again—so she voiced what was on her mind. "She's nothing like Mom."

thirteen

Bethany awoke the next morning determined to start the day on a positive note. All thoughts of Amanda Schnell had been thrust aside, and Ricky would soon be a distant memory.

She freed her legs out from under Willy, who had mimicked a cat comforter all night long, and padded to the bathroom barefoot.

While getting ready for work, Bethany switched from her beaded purse of the night before to her athletic bag. She retrieved her wallet, comb, and lipstick. Then she noticed the cocktail napkin snuggled against the satin lining. She pulled it out, giggling at the recollection of Cleo's encouraging suggestion to sell his autograph for a profit.

"I wonder how much I could get for it," she pondered, knowing it would go straight into her Brick Connor collection of memorabilia.

She turned the napkin over and caressed the bold signature. "This doesn't even look like his writing," she told her kitty, who was sprawled in unladylike fashion across the bed. Had Ricky changed his identity so much he actually became Brick Connor?

"What's this?" She noticed a slight bleed-through from writing on the inside of the folded napkin. There she found a personalized note that read: *My dearest Bethy, I've enjoyed our brief time together. It will not be another ten years before we see each other again. Yours forever, Ricky.*

She carefully folded the napkin and held it to her heart. Was this just another ring with a diamond chip setting? Something to appease her for another decade? *Please, Lord, no.*

❧

Brick had been back home in the Hollywood Hills about a month when Maggie called him from Alabama. When the cordless phone rang, he was sitting by his pool, reading a script for the next day.

"Hey, Brick." The gentle drawl that had tickled his ear when they first met now set his teeth on edge.

"Hi, Maggie."

"I haven't heard from you in a while."

"Sorry. We're finishing up this movie, working on studio stuff. Guess I've been too busy to keep in touch." What was he going to do? Even before seeing Bethany, he knew things were cooling off with Maggie—on his part anyway. Maggie had told him she would never yield to the Hollywood lifestyle. Short and numerous relationships were not for her. However, that meant she had chosen him for serious dating, apparently leading to marriage. He never should have let it go that far. The time apart, plus seeing Bethany again, cinched the deal. Now, how would he tell her?

Maggie sighed heavily into the phone. "We kick off the tour this weekend in my hometown. I'd love it if you'd come." Brick hesitated a second too long. Maggie continued. "I could show you around Florala. Then you could meet my momma and daddy." Yep, he should have said something before she threw down the *meet my folks* card. "You haven't tasted real Southern cookin' until you've eaten my momma's fried chicken and bread puddin'." Had her accent gotten thicker? How long had she been back home anyway?

"Look, Maggie. . . ." He didn't want to break up on the phone. But he had no time to run off to Alabama, either. He tried again. "Maggie, I've got something to tell you."

"What?" Her icy response told him she knew what was coming.

"I think we should cool it for a while." Silence. "Maggie?"

"Who is she?"

"Excuse me?"

Are all women so intuitive?

"Is it some sweet young thing you've chosen to *mentor*?"

He shook his head as if she could see through the receiver.

"It's just not working out. A relationship needs two people, ideally in the same area code."

Brick heard a shuddering sigh, intentionally loud enough to gain his sympathy. "I've put a lot of effort into trying to make this work. Apparently it's been one-sided all along."

He pressed two fingers to his closed eyelids. "Not one-sided, Mags. I just think things moved faster than I had anticipated."

Dead silence.

"Maggie?"

"You can't fool me, Brick." She spoke in an even, controlled tone. What happened to the shuddering sigh? "I know there's another woman, and you'll regret messing with me." He gripped the phone, tempted to throw it into the pool. "Go have your fling. You just blew your chance. Southern gals make terrific wives." A solid click assaulted his ear.

He glared at the now silent phone and slammed it to the table. Suddenly feeling the need to cool down, he peeled off his T-shirt and dove into the pool.

❧

Throughout the summer, Bethany found herself drawn into her routine. The film crew soon became a distant memory, and instead of rubbing elbows with Hollywood's elite, she found herself elbow deep in dead herring and squid. Instead of watching the talented actors work through their scenes, she watched her little finned troupe as she put them through their paces, day in and day out.

By midsummer, she had logged enough hours on her knees in prayer to qualify for mission work. Her future became a serious concern. No longer could she glide through life, particularly under her father's care. Amanda Schnell had begun to claim Glenn's time more each day, and Bethany could see she was losing him. It was only a matter of time before the two would get married, and then Bethany would be like a fifth wheel. She had to make plans now.

One evening, she sat on her bed with her knees pulled up under her chin. She enjoyed the therapy aspect of her job.

Maybe she should she go back to school to become a therapist, as Sheila had suggested. But after the Hollywood invasion, the call of the curtain seemed to niggle at the back of her mind constantly. Acting was in her blood.

Unbidden, a horrible memory surfaced. She was a teenager and had just opened the door to her home. . . .

Flashbulbs. Questions. "How does it feel to know your mother was in that tragic accident?" She didn't know. That was the first she'd heard.

Her father had whipped his sedan into the driveway and chased the reporters away, then held her long into the night.

The two sequestered themselves as much as possible, but those hounding reporters followed them through every step of the grieving process. Nothing was sacred—from the funeral plans to moving from their home in Beverly Hills. The headlines read FAMILY OF BELOVED ACTRESS, DEE BELLAMY, SELLS HOUSE TO PAY MOUNTING DEBT. There was no mounting debt. Mom simply wasn't there—the fire had died.

Eleven years later, the world had forgotten about Dee Bellamy. Grandma Bellamy was in a nursing home, her memory ravaged by Alzheimer's, and Bethany and her father had built a new life in Florida, blending in with the locals. No one ever suspected that they had been related to Hollywood royalty. Not even Cleo knew, a decision that Bethany had not made lightly. But Cleo was part of her new life.

When she saw Ricky, it all came flooding back. The photo shoots in the house, the publicity events, even visiting her mother on location during summer break. Bethany had been told she could follow in her mother's footsteps easily because she'd inherited her talent.

We could become a team like Taylor and Burton, Ricky's voice intruded. Was God bringing those thoughts into her head, or was it her own selfish desires? *I told you that you were a better actor than me.*

"Shut up, Ricky! You're not supposed to be on my mind when I'm praying!" Her outburst startled Willy, who, with enormous green eyes and a tail bushed out with fright, perched ready to flee. "I'm sorry, sweetheart," she cooed as she picked up the feline and stroked her long, soft fur. With apparent forgiveness, Willy emitted a pattering purr that pummeled her owner's chest with the feel of a carpeted jackhammer.

Ricky. He'd been gone a month, and she still hadn't heard from him. Fine. A relationship with him would only throw her back into the lifestyle she had left. She tried to shut out thoughts of him, but instead, the inevitable headlines assailed her imagination.

HOLLYWOOD HEARTTHROB AND BELLAMY DAUGHTER RECONNECT.

NEW DANGER ROLE FOR BRICK CONNOR AS HE PURSUES WEDDED BLISS.

HE SPIES, SHE SHIES—BRICK CONNOR TURNED DOWN FOR ROLE OF HUSBAND.

No, it was best that he was out of her life. No good could come from any kind of relationship with a man who lived in a glass house.

❧

Brick removed his suit and tie, throwing them onto the bed. The silk shirt came next. He hurled it toward the hamper, and it fell to a crumpled heap on the floor. After finding his sweatpants and favorite T-shirt under the bed, he tugged them on. The full-length mirror that doubled as his closet door reflected back a slovenly image. *This is me.*

Agitated from the talk show on which he had just been interviewed, he entered his kitchen in search of anything containing high carbohydrates.

"I'd give last year's salary for a chocolate bar right now," he grumbled as he searched through his refrigerator. What he found was caviar, liver pâté, and deboned meat from a Cornish game hen, all left over from a dinner party a couple of nights ago.

"Ah," he said after rooting through the freezer. "There is a God, and He has excellent taste in ice cream." He grabbed the half gallon of Super Fudgie Nutter, tossed the lid in the garbage, and grabbed a serving spoon from the drawer.

As he sat in front of his big-screen television, he snatched up the remote. Why he wanted to watch *The Ray Silverman Show*, he had no idea. It had been taped delayed and was scheduled to air in a few moments.

The host came out, did his ten-minute monologue, and then sat at his desk to introduce the first guest.

"And now, the man of *Danger*, Brick Connor."

Wild applause and female screams greeted Brick as he walked on from backstage. The band played a spy-sounding riff, and Brick lowered himself into the chair.

"Tell us, Brick; I'm sure everyone here is anxious to know. How many more *Danger* movies do you plan to do?"

"Well, Ray, after *Danger Down Under*, I'm contracted to do one more, but after that, I'm not so sure. Not getting any younger, you know."

Ray and the audience laughed. "You look in peak condition. Surely you can keep on going."

Brick chuckled. "Well, I'll be in my mid-thirties by the time the next one's done. It's a lot of physical work, so I don't know how long I can keep it up."

"We can't imagine anyone else in that role, can we, folks?" Ray tapped a pencil while the audience hooted their encouragement.

"Quite frankly, I'd like to move on to other things, something that will challenge my acting ability more."

"Are you saying you think the *Danger* series is fluff?"

Brick's knee started bouncing. "Let's just say that I haven't grown as an actor like I should have. Agent Danger's entire repertoire of emotions can be counted on two fingers."

"But it's an action role. You can't expect it to be Shakespeare."

"True, and don't get me wrong, this role has elevated my status in Hollywood considerably—"

"But," Ray interrupted, "you're unhappy."

Brick sighed. "Yeah, Ray, I guess you could say that. The quality of these movies has gone downhill, and I'm tired of it."

"I'd like to pursue this further, but I've got to take a commercial break." Ray looked straight at the camera. "We'll be back in a moment with more from Brick Connor."

The commercial showed a family running upstairs to get away from a burglar. The mother's face showed fright but softened to keep her children from panicking. The advertised alarm system shrilled, frightening away the would-be intruder.

"Even those actors have better roles than I do." Brick shoved a heaping spoonful of cold comfort into his mouth.

When the program came back on, Brick skillfully dodged the rest of Ray's questions. Or so he thought.

The phone rang, and the caller ID informed him it was his manager calling. He picked it up and began talking without saying hello.

"I know, Daryl, I have a big mouth."

"You're not making my job easy, Brick."

"Hey, he baited me. I'd have never spilled how unhappy I am on national television."

"But you did."

"Come on, how is it going to affect me? My contract is so solid even I can't get out of it. They can't fire me, can they?"

"That's not what I'm worried about. If you keep talking like this, it's going to get around that you're difficult to work with. Your writer's meetings have already been made public."

"If they didn't stink at their jobs, I wouldn't have to have meetings, would I? Why am I the bad guy here?"

"Because you're the star—and gaining a reputation of a spoiled star. Your agent can't get anything worthy of your talent after the *Danger* contract if you continue this kind of behavior. You avoid the reporters. You're standoffish at gatherings. You've even stopped playing the paparazzi. What's going on?"

Brick thought a moment. What *was* going on with him? Was it really an issue of wanting better roles? Was he tired of the Hollywood game? Or was it how he looked in Bethy's eyes? She'd made it clear she didn't want to be with Brick Connor, the movie star. She had nothing in common with that person.

That was why he hadn't called her. He didn't know how to win her over without using the old Brick charm, which was cheap and not worthy of a woman like Bethany.

"Brick?"

"Sorry, Daryl. I don't know what's going on with me. I think I need a vacation."

He heard Daryl's soft but anguished moan and knew his manager must be rubbing his eyebrow to relieve tension. Finally Daryl said, "Okay, you've been working nonstop for several years. We've built a stellar reputation. If you disappear for a month or two, it's not going to hurt us any. Just let me know where you are so I can send more scripts if any of your caliber come through."

The two men hung up, and Brick felt 100 percent better. First, because he liked Daryl, who knew what to say to stroke his ego, and second, because he gave him a great idea. He swirled what was left of the ice cream into a chocolate-nutter pudding and placed a dollop on his tongue. The cool, sweet dessert had changed its purpose. No longer comfort food, it was now something with which to celebrate.

He waved his spoon in the air as if directing an unseen orchestra. "I shall disappear."

❧

Bethany entered the gift shop, seeking out the air conditioning. The last of the tourists had left, and she craved not only a blast of cool air but also Cleo's brand of wacky humor.

However, when she stepped inside, she stopped before making her presence known. Cleo stood at the register counting the dollar bills slowly. The faraway look on her freckled face made her look like the subject of a Norman Rockwell painting.

Bethany stood watching her little friend for a full minute as Cleo counted the change. *Plink. . . Plink. . . Plink. . .* When she finally finished the quarters, Bethany moved toward her.

"Hey, girlfriend, what's up?"

Cleo leisurely looked up from her counting. A slow grin spread across her face. "I'm pregnant."

fourteen

"I'm so happy," Judy told Bethany after the auditions. "Since you've played the part of Rosalind twice before, I wouldn't trust it with anyone else." The director of *As You Like It* stuck a pencil in her hastily banded ponytail, apparently forgetting the two she already had in there.

It thrilled Bethany to be in the community auditorium again.

The next morning, Bethany woke refreshed. She opened her window and drew in a big breath. It had rained in the night, and the air smelled crisp, reminding her that autumn would soon paint the leaves yellow on the tree outside her window.

She reached for her robe that lay in her chair. Willy, who had curled up on it, glowered at her with one eye, the other buried somewhere beneath a furry paw. Bethany scooped her up and draped the limp body over her shoulder like a silk scarf. Willy protested weakly as Bethany began to dance around the room, pulling clothes from her closet.

After she had showered and dressed, she found Willy in a much better mood.

"Hungry?"

Willy's tail shot up and crooked on the end like a staff. With a flurry, Willy beat Bethany to the stairs and noiselessly maneuvered them. Bethany followed, rapping each wooden step with her sandaled feet.

She'd heard the teakettle whistle while still upstairs and knew her father had already started breakfast.

Willy reached the kitchen first but stopped abruptly, raised her middle, and turned to flee the way she had come. When the cat collided into her legs, Bethany had to fancy-dance to keep from crushing the black-and-white ball beneath her feet.

"What is wrong with you?"

Bethany extracted the cat from her ankles and carried her into the kitchen. She put the cat down and glanced at the figure sitting at the table, his face hidden behind a newspaper.

"Hey, Dad," she said after opening the refrigerator. "Do you have the orange juice behind that paper?"

"No. And you're about out of milk, too."

That was not her father's voice. She whirled, bumping her head, making the salad dressing bottles dance in the door.

"Hello, Bethy."

Slowly, the newspaper lowered to reveal the source of the voice that made her toes curl. She expected the dark, neatly groomed actor named Brick Connor to meet her gaping stare. However, the man leisurely enjoying the Saturday morning paper had a softer look, as if he'd suspended his workout routine. Tousled light brown hair brushed the top of wire-rimmed glasses that enhanced his—she looked closer—yes, forest green eyes.

When she finally managed to dislodge her heart from her throat, she croaked, "Rick—Bri—Ricky! What are you doing in my house?"

"I invited him." Her father sauntered into the kitchen as if a mega-box office star was not sitting at his table, drinking from his favorite mug, and reading his paper. Glenn held out a bakery box. "Muffin?"

❧

Brick had to steel himself from cracking a grin. Bethany looked so cute flustered. She stood there stammering, "But. . . Wha—I don't. . ."

"Ricky is taking a little vacation while researching a role, so I offered to let him stay in our guesthouse," Glenn explained.

He played his part very well. They had begun to plot on the night of the benefit but hadn't finalized the details. When Brick had his epiphany after talking to Daryl, he called Glenn, who then helped set up this scenario. They both knew the strategy of surprise, throwing the enemy off kilter and then moving in to conquer. He looked at Bethany's pale face. *Oh, she's off-kilter, all right.*

"Are you both crazy?" She grabbed her hair with both fists. Little blond tufts stuck out through her fingers, making her look like a rare, tropical bird.

The two men looked at one another and shrugged. Her father poured himself a cup of tea. "The man has to take a vacation somewhere; why not here?"

"Why not *here*? Why not simply invite the cameras in for a day in the life of an actor?" Her eyes suddenly widened, and she ran to the living room.

Brick picked up his mug and followed her. When he saw her peeking out of the drapes, he almost offered to forget the whole thing. He knew of her paparazzi phobia, but he had covered his tracks well.

"Relax." He flopped onto the sofa, already beginning to feel like Ricky—very comfortable in his girlfriend's house. "As far as Hollywood knows, I'm in Fiji, taking a well-deserved rest before I start my next project."

Bethany withered like a day-old dandelion. She sank into the chair across from him and dropped her head into her hands. "Won't they get suspicious when they can't find you there?"

"I sent my double. You remember Phillip? From the location shoot?"

She looked up and nodded. "Cleo and I couldn't believe the resemblance."

"There's a reason for that, beyond the obvious. Just as I can make myself look like Brick Connor, so can a dozen other men. Phillip is naturally dark, but he has my bone structure. We've fooled a few people over the years."

Bethany looked at him as if he'd lost his mind. She tilted her head slightly, her eyes seeking understanding. Maybe he had lost his mind, but he was a desperate man.

She drew in a breath, as if just now being able to expand her lungs after a basketball hit her in the gut. "You mentioned you were also studying for a role. What kind of role? Are you seeing how far you can go before you drive the heroine insane?"

Humor—good. Maybe he could get away with this. "I'm

researching what it would be like to be famous and yet live a normal life, out of the spotlight." He offered a smile that he hoped would be irresistible.

Bethany chewed on the corner of her mouth, and he wasn't sure if she believed him or not. In essence, it was true. Everything an actor did went straight into his toolbox.

The cat he'd frightened that morning daintily picked her way to her owner's lap where she began smacking and washing her face. Apparently Glenn had fed her. Brick reached over and plucked the feline from Bethany's lap. The fur ball purred as if she'd known him all her life.

Bethany's lips turned up slightly as she regarded her pet in his arms. "Traitor."

❧

Ricky gazed deep into Willy's eyes. "This isn't Moose, is it?" The whole thing felt surreal to Bethany. Why was she talking to this man about her cat? She should be throwing him out on his ear.

"No, it's her daughter, Willy."

His rich laugh tickled the inside of her stomach. "Okay, I remember Moose was a nickname for Shamu. If you followed tradition and named her for famous killer whales, I'd say this one is. . ." He thought for a moment, continuing to look deep into Willy's eyes, as if the answer could be seen in there. "No, you didn't." Bethany shot what she hoped was a solid glare. "You named your cat after the whale in the movie *Free Willy*?"

Glenn, who walked in from the kitchen, joined the conversation. "My daughter is nothing if not imaginative."

"Remember that gray kitten she had years ago?" Ricky talked as if she weren't in the room.

"She named him Flipper." Her father's eyes twinkled with mischief. "All the other little girls had kittens named Fluffy and Whiskers." Both men let loose with belly laughs.

Bethany sat up straight. "You two think you're cute, don't you? This will never work."

"Sure it will." Ricky put Willy down. "You may have noticed that my appearance has been altered." He lifted his hands and rotated for a full view. "This is what Ricky O'Connell would have looked like if he hadn't become. . ." He struck a pose that looked more like a 007 shtick than his own character. "Brick Connor—Man of Danger." He wriggled his eyebrows in a swarthy manner.

Bethany let a giggle escape. She pointed to the couch. "Sit down, Dangerous, and let's figure this out."

She allowed herself a closer look. He was far from the dark, handsome star who had escorted her to the benefit three months ago. He now wore sweatpants in the purple and gold colors of the Los Angeles Lakers and a faded T-shirt he had apparently slept in. "What did you do to yourself?"

"I quit working out and drank a few milk shakes."

"A few?" She glanced at his midsection.

"Hey, don't get personal." He patted the offended tummy. "It may not be rock hard anymore, but it's far from looking like a bowl full of jelly." Then he stroked his head, flattening a stubborn cowlick. "Also, I had the hairdresser strip the dark color off and then dye it back. Did you know they don't make a dye for dirty blond? This was as close as I could get."

She found it quite attractive. Gold highlights in soft, longish hair, grown out from the snappy, gelled look of the actor. And the wire glasses were much more stylish than those awful, black plastic ones of his youth. The missing mustache made his clean-shaven face look younger. He was more approachable— *more Ricky*. Maybe it could work. He was, after all, researching an upcoming role. Certainly she could help. Still, her initial reservations clung to her like a pit bull.

"I don't know." There would be no peace if he were found out. Up until a few years ago, people still talked about the accident that took Dee Bellamy's life. She had endured it on the anniversary of her death every year. "Aren't you putting us all in jeopardy? You're sure to be recognized."

"You know," Ricky continued to present his case, "people will only see what they want to see."

"I don't understand."

"Have you ever seen someone you knew in a totally different

place than you were used to seeing them, and you couldn't quite place them because they didn't belong there?"

Glenn helped out. "Like the time we saw Mrs. Killinger at Disney World on vacation. At church, we would have recognized her instantly."

"Oh yeah." Bethany nodded. "But in the different surroundings, I couldn't place her." She wrinkled her nose. "It was the first time I'd ever seen her in shorts."

Glenn grunted in agreement from his recliner.

"Yes!" Ricky said. "That's exactly what I'm talking about."

"But you're a big celebrity. One who has been here filming recently. Wouldn't it make sense for them to figure you out?"

He stood, took hold of her hands, and shook them for emphasis. "People see only what they want to see."

She pulled away, self-conscious at his touch.

"Why would Brick Connor be acting like a real person with other real people? Believe me, they will buy the fact that I'm an old friend of the family, just visiting. It makes more sense."

"How can you be so sure?"

"How do you think I got from one coast to another without so much as a whimper in the news?"

"You mean you've done this before?"

"Remember when I followed you around at work? Even you didn't recognize me. I'm an actor; I can play different roles. Give me a pair of sunglasses, cutoff jeans, and a three-day-old beard. You can't tell me from any other working stiff."

She drew her shoulder up to her cheek in an effort to shut out what was beginning to sound like common sense.

"Trust me. At the first sign of a camera, or nosy reporter, I'm out of here." He slid to one knee in front of her and again took her hands in his. "Give me a chance, Bethy. Let me prove to you that I'm still Ricky. And even though that Brick character intruded, Bethany Rae Hamilton and Patrick Richard O'Connell deserve a second chance."

fifteen

Why was she taking this chance? Distracted didn't even begin to describe Bethany that day, knowing she was harboring a movie star. Since Ricky's arrival that morning, she feared everyone knew. Every tourist seemed suspicious, as if they all wore press badges under their gaudy shirts. She was even afraid to confide in Cleo for fear someone might overhear. What if the gift shop were bugged?

The next morning, she wished she'd made an effort to give Cleo a heads-up. The quick "We need to talk" while they were putting on their robes didn't hack it. When they filed into the choir loft at the front of the church and turned to face the congregation, her friend choked on her first note at the sight of the altered actor sitting next to Glenn.

During announcements, Cleo leaned toward her and whispered, "Is that who I think it is?" Bethany preoccupied herself with the bulletin to avoid having to look up.

Heat rose from the yoke on her choir robe, and she knew she must be turning several shades of crimson. "He said no one would recognize him." She stole a glance in his direction and found him watching her, with a silly smirk on his face and an impish twinkle in his eye. She looked back down at the bulletin and wrung it like a dishrag.

"What's he doing here?"

The other choir members were all within earshot, so Bethany whispered back, "I can't talk here. Can you come over after church? I need an ally." Then, to their extreme horror, the pastor asked for all the visitors to stand and introduce themselves.

"He wouldn't!" Bethany hissed.

He didn't.

But her father did. "Pastor," he stood and made his announcement, sounding much like his trumpet, "I'd like to introduce an old friend of the family. He's here from California for a few weeks of R & R."

Ricky stood, and Bethany was forced to play a part harder than any in her acting career. As two hundred faces seemed to swivel her way, she forced herself to sit straight and smile as if she were happy to have company from back home.

Pastor Wilkes only made the matter worse. "Welcome. What's your name?"

"My friends call me Ricky."

He glanced at Bethany. She jerked her gaze to the mangled, now-unrecognizable, bulletin.

"Well, Ricky," the pastor said, "welcome on behalf of Safe Harbor Community Church."

The service continued, and Cleo tugged on the sleeve of Bethany's robe. "Look at the people, Bethany."

"What?" She forced herself to look up from her lap.

"*Look.* No one recognizes him."

Bethany scanned the congregation. Not one person stared or pointed in the star's direction. Not one seemed flustered while searching out a pen for an autograph. They were all acting normal. She felt her heart begin to slow its patter and the blood subside from her cheeks. Could he have been right? A little alteration and no one knows who he is? She prayed with all her heart that God would place them in a time warp so they could get to know one another again.

How long will it last, Lord?

To her surprise, the answer came quickly. *As long as it takes.*

Standing outside the church and greeting her friends felt like a study in human behavior. Erin, a friend from choir, approached with her husband and two children in tow.

"How nice to have company, Bethany. Did you go to school together?"

A million answers zinged inside her head, all betraying Ricky's identity, her feelings for him, or anything that would reveal her past life. She finally decided on three simple words. "Yes. . .we did."

Ricky came to her rescue. "Bethany and I have known each other a long time. When the opportunity presented itself for me to visit, I jumped at it."

Erin's husband joined the conversation while trying to keep his two-year-old daughter from sticking a lollipop in his hair. "How long will you be with us?"

"I've had a break in my work schedule, so it will probably be several weeks."

"What do you do?"

What an innocent question. Bethany held her breath waiting for the answer.

"I do studio work—pictures."

"Oh, a photographer. Do you do baby pictures? We'd love to have a good one of little Marissa." He tickled the baby's tummy, and she giggled.

"Sorry, I don't have the right equipment here." Ricky held out his hand to the baby, and she wrapped her pudgy fingers around his thumb.

Erin touched her husband's arm. "He's on vacation, dear." She gave Ricky an apologetic smile.

Ricky pulled his now-sticky thumb away from the baby while her father said, "I'm sorry, you said that in church, didn't you?" He put the baby down, and she began to fuss. "Well, it's nap time. Nice to have you with us."

On the way home, Bethany fumed in the front seat of the Blazer while Glenn drove. She twisted around to confront Ricky sitting behind her father.

"A photographer?" Sarcasm dripped from every syllable. "I never would have agreed to this if I'd known you were going to lie to my friends."

Ricky shrugged. "Hey, I didn't lie. I told him exactly what I do for a living. He made an assumption."

"But then you said your equipment wasn't here."

"I said I didn't have the right equipment. That's true, too."

"That's a gray area, and you know it." How had he gotten so far away from God's truth? The teenage Ricky would have known absolutes.

"Would you rather I told everyone the exact truth? In my career, I've learned diplomacy—when to back off and when to be straightforward. I've even learned when to fudge the truth. It's called survival."

Bethany raised her eyes heavenward. "God help us all."

Later, Bethany and Cleo put sandwiches and sodas on a tray and took them to the enclosed patio out back.

"How's your husband?" Ricky asked Cleo. "I never did get to meet him."

"He's overseas again. Due back in January, a month before the baby is born."

"And I thought my career was tough."

"You get used to it. Knowing he's keeping us safe is reward enough, and of course, I pray for him constantly." Cleo's smile lost its sparkle. Bethany knew she missed her husband horribly.

Cleo tilted her chin, resembling a little redheaded bird. "You know, you look smaller somehow. Is that an illusion?"

"Cleo!" Bethany couldn't believe her friend's boldness.

Ricky's hearty laugh made her feel better. "The illusion is the character I play. He's larger than life on the big screen. So when I show up as Brick Connor, they see me as this six-foot action figure. But when I become just another ordinary guy, I'm not as imposing."

"That makes sense."

"I've got this changing-roles-back-and-forth thing down to a science." He winked at Bethany and took a bite of his sandwich. "Mmm. You know, I haven't had egg salad in years. You make it just like your mom."

Bethany felt a sting of a tear. Ever since Ricky showed up at work several months ago, he brought with him all the memories she had pushed down deep. She thought she had conquered her grief, but his presence peeled off a bandage to expose the wound that had never quite healed.

"Do you remember when we had that party at your house?" Ricky asked.

"The one the football team crashed?"

"Yeah!"

Glenn looked at Cleo. "We had dozens of parties at our house. It's eerie that they know exactly which one."

"You see," Ricky said to Cleo, "we had the entire cast and crew of *The Music Man* at Bethy's house."

Bethany's cheeks warmed. Did he have to call her that in public? Cleo raised an eyebrow. The endearment had not slipped by her.

"We had completed the last performance," Ricky continued. "Most of us were still in makeup, and I was wearing the striped jacket."

Bethany got into the spirit and continued the tale. "We were deep into our chips and sodas, watching the home video my dad made. We were laughing at ourselves and acting silly, remembering when we flubbed and what was happening backstage, when the doorbell rang. In walked the roughest jocks you've ever seen, expecting to make fun of us and walk out with all of our snacks."

Cleo looked at Glenn. "Where were you?"

"We had discreetly removed ourselves to the back of the house. At their age they didn't need us hovering." He popped a potato chip into his mouth and crunched.

Ricky took up the story. "At that moment, on the tape, we were singing "Ya Got Trouble," and as if on cue, we all turned to the jocks—and started singing it to them." He wiped a tear, barely able to contain himself. "Now understand, at school, we would cringe when these guys walked by, but at Bethy's house, we were in our element. We started singing and dancing around them."

At that point, the two began to dance around the patio, lifting their hands to the ceiling. Ricky never missed a consonant as he sang about trouble with a capital T.

Cleo giggled while protectively holding her extended tummy. "I think I know how those poor guys felt."

Bethany flopped onto the wicker couch, her energy spent. "You should have seen their faces. We wouldn't let them go. We just dragged them into our world, and before long, they were doing that cadence where the townspeople all chant "trouble." They were actually enjoying themselves." She slapped Ricky on the arm. "They stayed for the whole party. One of them even went out for more snacks. It was a riot!"

✿

"The halls at school were much friendlier after that," Ricky said. "They nicknamed me Harold and would chant "trouble" whenever they saw me."

When they were able to get their breath, Ricky said to Cleo, "You know, I'm glad you're in on our secret. I think having backup will settle Bethy's mind."

"I won't blow your cover." She briefly glanced at Bethany. "In fact, I'll pray for you while you're here incognito. God may have a plan for you in all of this subterfuge."

Bethany said a silent prayer herself. *Please, Lord, bring back the prodigal.*

"Thank you, Cleo," Ricky said. "It's appreciated more than you know."

That evening, long after Cleo had left, Ricky and Bethany continued to reminisce. She had gotten out her box of high school memories, minus the candy box with the ring. They rummaged through them as if the box were a treasure chest full of rare and precious jewels.

"I can't believe you still have that." He held up a small stuffed toy he had won for her in one of those claw machines at the mall. "It cost me five dollars to win that for you."

"And it's only worth a quarter." She smiled at the little blue dolphin, whose left eye hung precariously. She never expected the cheap toy to last more than a few years, but it had found a loving home in her memory box.

The two sat on the floor, where they had room to toss

contents as they looked at them. When he noticed the high school annual from their senior year, he moved to the couch and turned on the lamp next to it. Bethany followed him to look over his shoulder.

After adjusting his glasses, he turned the pages tenderly. "I haven't thought of these people in years." Bethany let him get lost in the past. After a while he said, "You know, sometimes I wish we were back there again."

"What do you mean? Would you live those years with your father over again?"

He winced, and she saw him rub the scar on his chin. She wished she hadn't brought up that part of his past. "No, but the time I spent at your house to get away from him is something I'll always cling to in my memories. I have never felt more love than in your home."

Bethany pulled her legs to her chin and hugged them. "My mom had that gift."

He turned to look at her. "It wasn't just your mom." Appearing to weigh his next words, he placed his arm behind her on the couch but never touched her. His spicy scent swirled around Bethany, and her heart started beating a familiar rhythm. After a moment, Ricky said, "I have never felt the kind of love we had."

ða

Ricky searched Bethany's face. Did she understand? Two transparent emerald pools gazed back at him, at first placid but then whirling as her apparent emotions registered what he had just said.

She looked away quickly. "But that was kid stuff. We didn't know anything about love."

He felt a knot in his gut the size of a fist. Surely she wasn't telling him those years together meant nothing. He ventured a touch, just light fingers on her opposite shoulder. He saw her tense but was encouraged when she didn't pull away. She closed her eyes and swallowed; then he felt the tremble. Ah, that was what he wanted. Some indication that she still felt something for him. He pulled his arm back into his own territory and started turning pages again.

Out of the corner of his eye, he saw her squirm and shove her hands under her thighs.

"Ricky. How do you feel about God now?"

❧

Bethany gauged his reaction. How far had he gotten from the Word? Would he be angry? Would he lash out? If they had any future at all, she had to know where his heart was.

He looked at her with pain in his eyes. "I'm so unworthy. How could He love someone like me?"

Was this Brick Connor, who captured a room with his presence? Who commanded every conversation and seemed so self-assured that his very demeanor demanded respect? No, this was Ricky O'Connell, troubled by a turbulent childhood, guilty over the sins of his father. Still doubting, even though he had asked God into his heart years ago, that someone could love him unconditionally.

A trilling Gershwin tune broke the spiritual moment. Ricky grabbed the persistent cell phone from the side table next to the couch. After a quick glance at the caller ID, he said, "I'm sorry; I have to take it. I've been waiting all weekend for this call."

She began to lift herself off the couch to give him some privacy, but he motioned for her to stay. After a moment of listening to the one-sided argument, she deduced it to be business.

He stood and began pacing. "No. . .tell him to keep searching, okay? No. . .I don't want to play another spy. Get me out of this typecast, will you? . . . I don't know, maybe a bad-guy role this time. How about the dredge of society, somebody they'll love to hate? Or maybe a recovering alcoholic, something with meat?" Bethany saw him tense and knew the conversation had taken a turn for the worse. "No, I can't do that. . . . I don't care what you promised. . . . You have my timetable; work around it." He took a deep breath. "Look, just send me what you've got, and I'll look at them. But I'm not making any promises. . . . Yeah, the address I gave you. . . I'll let you know when I'm back. . . . Thanks, you're a good man. . . . Hug that wife for me. . . . Bye."

He flipped the tiny phone shut and turned to Bethany. "My manager."

"I guessed that."

"He's sending me some scripts from my agent to look through. Don't worry." He must have seen on her face the slight alarm that she felt. "He'll send it to Phillip, who will forward it here. He also wanted me to fly back for a promotional thing. Just a quickie, then I could fly back."

"Does he think you're in Fiji?" She lifted a brow.

He cleared his throat and shuffled his feet. "Well, yeah. He thought I'd be partying with my rowdy friends. . .or with a girl."

"You are with a girl," she teased, knowing exactly what he meant.

He sat back down. "Well, Daryl isn't one for propriety. He'll call anytime, day or night."

"Sundays, as well, I assume." She sat with one leg pulled under and tapped the knee of the leg touching the floor.

"Daryl never rests. Irene calls him the workaholic from. . ." He looked away. "Anyhow, he's good at what he does. He's been working this promotional deal for weeks, but I don't want to do it."

"Why not?" She looked at his altered appearance, wondering if it would be hard to change back.

"I would have to cut my vacation short. Let's just say. . ." He sat up straight, removed his glasses, and allowed Brick to say his next words. "I don't want to leave Fiji just yet."

sixteen

"Bethany."

"Mom?"

"Bethany honey, time for school. 'This is the day the Lord has made; let us rejoice and be glad in it.'"

Bethany awoke with a start, searching her room for her mother. It had been years since she'd had these dreams.

After a night of intermittent sleep, she managed to drag herself through another day of work. She was grateful that her last therapy session was with Emily, an eight-year-old child with Down syndrome. She loved Emily, who was no stranger to the routine. After several sessions with Cocoa, she had improved her motor skills and begun to talk more intelligibly.

Emily entered the Encounter building with her mother and ran up to Sheila, wrapping her chubby arms around her waist. "Hi, She-ah." She waved to Bethany, who waited for her by the pool. "Hi, Befany."

"Hi, Emily." Bethany waved her over. "Are you ready to go swimming?"

Emily clapped her hands and began a singsong, "Co-coa. . . Co-coa. . .Co-coa."

Emily's mother was a large woman whose belly laugh could be heard over the barking seals. "That means yes."

Bethany recalled the first time they saw this overzealous child, over a month ago. It took effort to keep her on the step and not allow her to plunge in with the dolphin. Over time, Emily realized she wouldn't really be *swimming* with Cocoa. She'd made much progress, and if things went well today, it would probably be her last session, to Bethany's regret.

Sheila spoke to the child as they sat together in the pool. "Say my name, Emily."

When Emily could say Sheila's name correctly, she was allowed to give Cocoa a command. She placed two fingers to her lips, and the dolphin bobbed out of the water to give her a kiss. Then Sheila asked her to say her own name, Emily, since it was the letter *L* that she had such a hard time with. Both therapist and trainer encouraged the little girl with laughter. It seemed more like party time than work.

After several exercises with blended sounds, such as *three, think,* and *bath,* Bethany called out from the middle of the pool. "Say *my* name, Emily." Emily had been taught that if she could say the *th* sound, Cocoa would pull Bethany around the pool. At the end, Cocoa would wave her fluke.

Emily screwed her plump face until it looked like a raisin, put her lips together for the beginning of the name, and let it fly. "Beh-THA-ny!"

"Who-oo!" Bethany signaled Cocoa to slip under her arm, and the two swished around the pool. She gave Emily an extra treat by letting go early and *telling* Cocoa to do a flip.

"Co-coa. . .Beh-thany. . .Co-coa. . .Beh-thany. . ."

When the session ended, Sheila determined this would indeed be Emily's last one. Bethany knelt to be eye level with the wet moppet, who had mummified herself in a large beach towel. "Come visit me, okay?" She looked up at Emily's mother. "Seriously, anytime you're here, have someone find me if you don't see me right away. I don't know what I'd do if I missed a hug from this big girl." Her reward was a fierce squeeze around her neck.

By the time Bethany returned home that evening, she was tired enough to go to bed without supper but found she'd rather put off falling asleep. Would these recurring dreams of her mother prompt the one about the hissing snakes, striking at her with flashes of light outside her door in California?

She found Ricky on the computer in the little office. The sight of him helped jump-start her energy. She wondered fleetingly if she could keep him there indefinitely and turn him into a househusband.

As if he knew her thoughts, he greeted her, "Hi, honey, how

was your day? Supper will be ready in a jiffy; we're grilling tonight."

She flopped into the overstuffed armchair by the desk and teased, "You need to get out more. Is this what you do all day? Or do you spend some of your time watching soap operas?"

"Nah, when they turned me down for a role on *The Dead and the Listless*, it soured me on them." He continued to click the keyboard. "Did you know that there are at least ten Web sites dedicated to my career?" He began naming them off on his fingers. "There's the Brick Connor Official Web Site, the Brick Connor—Man of Danger Web Site, the I Love Brick Connor Web Site, the Hey, Brick, Be Dangerous with Me Web Site. . . ."

"Enough! So you're popular; didn't you know that?"

"Well, yeah, but I never thought I was an obsession. I talked to some of these people today."

Bethany's eyes popped wide open. "How?"

"In a chat room. They didn't know it was me, so they talked normal, not stuttering and flustered like I'm used to."

She shook her head. "I don't believe this."

"It was cool. I used the name Danger Disciple, and I found out all kinds of things."

"I'm afraid to ask."

"For instance, some of them like Agent Danger's hair better in the first movie than the second. One guy told me he thought the gadgets my character used were more realistic than most spy shows, but he liked James Bond's cars better."

"Well, there's no beating the Aston Martin." She smiled at his enthusiasm.

"I agree there. You know, I've been upset over the thin plot in the last two movies. And there's little hope for the rest. Everyone in the chat room agreed with me."

Bethany scooted to the edge of the chair. "Are you trying to cause an uprising? Don't you want people to go see your movies?"

"Of course; that's the point. They'll stop if things don't change." He took off his glasses and rubbed his eyes. Bethany wondered how long he'd been sitting there. "Don't you see? If

I complain, I look like a spoiled prima donna. But if the fans rebel or, as you put it, start an uprising, maybe someone will listen." He sat back in the swivel desk chair and chuckled. "I gave them an address to voice their concerns."

He sat there a moment, absently looking at the monitor with his knee bouncing slightly. Something was on his mind.

"Bethy, how long do you intend to be a dolphin trainer? Have you ever considered coming home and starting your own career in show business?"

&

"How long do I intend to be a dolphin trainer?" She repeated through closed teeth.

Uh-oh. He must have hit a nerve.

"You say that as if it were nothing more than an after-school job. My father has made a very good living at it, you know."

"And your mother was a very good actress. You have her genes, too. Why are you wasting your talents here?"

"Wasting my talents? Just today, a beautiful little girl hugged my neck and said my name, *clearly,* for the first time. That's what I do, Ricky. That's where I make a difference."

"Did you do it, or did the therapist do it? Who made the difference?" He wasn't trying to be argumentative, but with Bethany's unique gift, he couldn't understand why she chose this line of work. There were hundreds in the entertainment field who didn't have half her talent.

"Without me, Sheila couldn't do her job. I'm the reason Emily wants to try harder."

"Come on, any trainer could do what you do. But only Bethany Hamilton can follow in her mother's footsteps. Come back with me and take up where your mom left off."

She pushed herself deeper into the chair. Her eyes had suddenly turned wild, as if a pack of dogs were nipping at her heels. "I. . .can't."

"Or maybe you won't." Now was the time to say what had been on his mind since first arriving in Florida. "Maybe you prefer to continue what you're doing as an excuse to live at home, under your father's wing."

She closed her eyes and balled a tuft of hair in her fist. *That's it, isn't it, Bethy? You're hiding behind your father.*

He spoke to her in what he hoped was a comforting tone. "Bethy, look at me." When she did, he continued. "At the risk of playing an armchair therapist, consider this. Because of your mom's sudden death, you've developed a dependence on the one parent remaining. If you hadn't moved to Florida, I might have been able to take up that slack and help you move on with your life." At least, that's what he'd hoped. They would have married, and he would have protected her for the rest of her life. It wasn't too late for that. He just had to convince her.

Bethany slowly uncurled her body in the chair. She placed her hands on the arms and said, "So, you've made yourself my savior. Where were you those ten years? It was God who kept me sane during that awful time. He was the One who spoke to me when you wouldn't call. He was the One who held me when I heard you were having yet another fling. What happened to you, Ricky? I know you accepted Christ—I was there. Or was that just more playacting? Before telling me what I should do with my life, maybe you should look deep inside yourself. There's a big, black void in there, and only God's love can fill it."

She stood up and walked toward the door. "You said we were grilling. I'll make the salad."

He turned his back to her but nodded. When he knew she had left, he took off his glasses and rubbed his burning eyes.

❧

Bethany ran warm water over the dishrag. Her thoughts turned to the argument before supper. Why was he pushing her? Would he risk demeaning her chosen profession just to get her to move back home? *Home.* She pitched the rag at the kitchen table. That was his word, not hers. California was no longer home. *I belong here, with Dad.* That thought drew her up short. Could Ricky be right? Was she clinging to her father?

She heard the telephone ring once and knew Glenn had

picked it up right away. Must have been someone he knew on the caller ID.

Ricky walked into the kitchen as she began to wipe the table. He opened the dishwasher and asked, "Can I help?"

She barely glanced at him. "Our arrangement was when you cook, I clean. Weren't you going to play chess with Daddy?"

He placed a dish in the machine and proceeded to rinse another. "He just got a phone call. I think it's his lady friend. They'll probably talk all night."

Bethany's stomach knotted. *Amanda.*

Ricky continued. "I want to apologize for my earlier remark." He placed the last glass in the dishwasher, poured soap in the special container on the door, and locked it up tight.

When the machine started humming and swishing, Bethany said, "Let's take a walk, get away from this noisy thing."

A balmy breeze blew from the Gulf, and Bethany could smell the salt in the air. Although the sun had gone down some time ago, the temperature was still a comfortable seventy-five degrees. She glanced at Ricky and asked, "You up for ice cream?"

"Sure." He patted his belly. "Don't have to worry about carbs right now."

They headed for the center of town, strategically placed by the developers of Seaside to be within walking distance of the entire community. At the ice cream shop, they ordered a couple of sundaes and then sat outside at a small table. No other patrons were near, so the setting felt intimate.

Ricky swirled the chocolate sauce with his spoon, but before he ate a bite, he said, "I'm sorry. I had no right telling you what to do."

Bethany spooned a small bite into her mouth, the sweet strawberry coolness soothing her ego as much as Ricky's words just now. She had feared her words had been a bit harsh, too, and was grateful for his forgiving nature toward her. "I'd like a second opinion on your diagnosis of my psyche." She offered a tiny grin as a truce offering. "But I do accept your apology, if you'll accept mine."

"Bethy, not everyone is as committed to God as you and your father. I admit, I had a wild side shortly after fame hit, but I've settled down quite a bit."

"Yes, you have. Christianity is a process, and we don't all mature at the same levels. All I ask is that you seek God concerning your career and personal life."

Ricky poked at his sundae. "I have a lot of junk to sort out. I guess I've kept it on the back burner, not wanting to deal with it. Maybe I'm still not ready to deal with it."

"God cares, Ricky. Let Him help you."

When she noticed his jaw clench, she sensed she'd pushed too far and changed the subject. "Since you're playing the role of psychiatrist, how's this? For the last four nights, I've dreamed of my mom. What do you make of that, doctor?"

Apparently he accepted the change of mood, and Bethany marveled at his ability to take on a new role. He pulled his glasses to the tip of his nose and looked over them at her. With a bad Austrian accent, he said, "Vell, vhat ve have here iss a transference of brain waves calling up memories—pictures, if you vill—brought on by an outside influence, causing an automatic response that stimulates said pictures, thereby playing them during REM, vhich is a time vhen the brain is vulnerable to unvanted stimuli." She must have given him a vacant look, because he translated. "I am causing your dreams." He pushed his glasses back up his nose and took another bite of ice cream.

"Huh?"

"It's simple, really. You associate your youth with me, and your mom was part of your youth."

"But why didn't I have these dreams when you were here filming?" She glanced around to be sure they couldn't be heard.

"Because I wasn't Ricky."

That made sense. Brick Connor wouldn't kick off old memories, because he'd never been in her life before. And now, here was Ricky, talking about the old days. She hoped by solving the mystery that it would stop the dreams.

They finished their ice cream and set out for home.

seventeen

"I hate to leave you home alone tonight. You've only been here a few days, and already I'm deserting you." Bethany grabbed her bag and slung it over her shoulder. She had talked to her guest for too long that morning and found herself running late for work.

Ricky looked up from the toast he was buttering. "Don't worry about it. I know how important choir practice is. Maybe I'll take your advice and get myself out of the house."

She clutched the keys in her hand, wincing at the sharp pain when they dug into her palm. "I was only kidding, you know. There's no use in calling attention to yourself. Maybe I should come straight home; they can do without me for a few practices."

Ricky stood up and escorted her to the door. "I'll be careful. Didn't I prove myself Sunday? Where's your faith?" He kissed her head and shoved her out of the house.

As she stood on the front porch staring at the now closed door, she swallowed hard. Where *was* her faith? Why did she have to second guess everything? Hadn't God already given her peace about allowing Ricky back into her life? She knew He had a plan, but she sure wished He'd let her in on it.

That evening, when she and Cleo walked into the sanctuary, she wondered again about what God might be doing to her when she saw Ricky there—sitting in the choir loft, with a folder of his own!

Gladys, the choir director, was all smiles. "Bethany! You didn't tell me you were hiding this treasure."

Bethany felt the color drain from her face and feared Cleo might have to catch her.

Gladys continued to gush. "Ricky sang a few bars for us just before you came in. He wasn't sure what part he sang." She turned back to Ricky. "You have a beautiful baritone voice. Very polished. Where did you train?"

Ricky's eyes sparkled as he said, "I haven't had any formal training except for high school. Bethany and I were in choir together there."

"Well, you have natural talent then." Gladys pointed to the seat next to Ricky. "Bethany, you can sit next to your friend and show him the ropes. Bass and altos in back, tenors and sopranos in front."

First the surprise appearance in her kitchen, and now this. She leaned toward him and whispered, "You've got to stop. You're going to affect my heart."

He turned, his lips an inch from her ear. "That's what I'm trying to do."

⋙

When rehearsals started two days later for *As You Like It*, Ricky knew he was making progress when Bethany invited him along. She stood there, with her hands on her hips, so cute he had to restrain himself from picking her up and swinging her around the living room. "I can't take any more surprises. You've convinced me you can stay incognito. But. . ." She pointed her finger and wagged it in his direction. "You're going to have to promise to be good and just hang out. You are not to be a part of this production. Someone will see through you for sure."

"I promise."

Ricky tried to make good his oath, but when the set director needed an extra pair of hands to build the forest, he couldn't just sit there. Soon he hammered and painted with gusto.

By the second week, the sets were beginning to shape up, and the actors had shed their scripts.

"Where's Jared?" Judy asked the company. They all looked at one another and shrugged. "I wanted to run through Act 3, Scene 2, but I guess we can skip the verses where Orlando places love poems on the trees and begin where Corin and Touchstone enter."

As the two men positioned themselves onstage, a woman ran in from the back of the auditorium. "Bad news, y'all. Jared broke his leg."

Over the gasps, Judy's strangled voice asked, "What about his understudy?"

"Stan was with him. They were on a Jet Ski, and it crashed. Stan broke his collarbone."

Judy clutched the glasses hanging on a chain around her neck and dramatically sank into a theater chair. "What are we going to do? We can't cast someone at such late notice."

Ricky hopped off the stage, where he had been fixing a tottering tree. He walked past Bethany without looking at her and cleared his throat.

❊

Bethany watched Ricky stride past her as if in a dream. By the set of his jaw and the determination in his eyes, she knew what he was about to do.

"Ahem. . ."

No!

"I played Orlando in high school. After watching the rehearsal, most of it has come back to me."

Whispers ranged from inaudible white noise to "But does he have talent?"

"We have no choice." Judy clutched her notebook and started patting her pockets. The assistant director reached over and plucked a pencil from the director's ponytail.

Heaven, help me. Bethany should have tied him to the table at home. She should have hobbled his ankles like they do horses. She should have thrown him out of her house weeks ago, but she never had the strength. Truth be told, she liked having him there.

"Bethany." Judy chewed on the pencil. "What do you think?"

"S—sure. He was good in school. And like you said, what choice do we have?"

"Great! Ricky, are you ready, or would you rather take some time to study while we rehearse another?"

"Oh, I feel comfortable, as long as I can use the script my first few times out."

"Okay, here's the scene, and here are your props. I assume you know what to do with them."

He smiled like a schoolboy given an important assignment. He then launched into Act 3, Scene 2, and became Orlando, mewling his lovesickness for the fair Rosalind and placing poems on the trees he had just set up. "Hang there, my verse, in witness of my love."

❧

"Lord, what are You doing to me?"

As Bethany waited by the indoor interaction pool for her customer, she watched Cocoa move effortlessly through the water. So calm, so serene. Watching the glistening animal suspended in her world, floating without a care, brought Bethany's stress level down considerably.

She prayed that Jared and Stan would heal quickly. However, last night's shock wasn't so much about their accident as more about Ricky.

Lord, please don't let his cover be blown before I've had a chance to talk more about You. She realized her little tirade of the other night was not real witnessing, but rather a dodge to get out from under Ricky's uncomfortable microscope. Yes, he needed to search his heart, but she needed to be more sensitive.

She found herself thanking God for her many blessings, including the second chance He'd given her with Ricky. She closed her eyes and prayed for wisdom. *Lord, please don't let my quick temper and loose tongue destroy what it's taken You ten years to build.*

"Now, that's a beautiful picture."

She nearly fell into the pool when she started at the familiar voice. "You're doing it again! Why are you here?"

He looked at his watch. "I have an appointment."

"*You* booked the encounter? Why didn't you tell me?"

Ricky laughed. "I like seeing you rattled. It fluffs my ego."

"Your ego doesn't need fluffing."

She led him to the wet suits and showed him where to change. When he came out, she stole a glance at his muscled torso. If this was his idea of letting himself go, she wondered what he thought peak condition might be.

Normally there would be a small audience to watch the encounter, family members or others simply curious about the training process. Today, however, they had the building to themselves, and she found herself thankful for her own wet suit. It discreetly covered her in all the right places and made her feel better about any impropriety. They weren't teenagers in the backyard pool anymore.

They sat on the step under the water, and a toothy grin surfaced before them. "Ricky O'Connell, meet Cocoa."

He placed his palm on the surface of the water and Cocoa swam under it for a pat. "Pleased to meet you, Cocoa."

Bethany cocked her head. "Looks like you still remember what I taught you back home."

"Like riding a bicycle. I remember how my friends were so jealous that not only did I have the most beautiful girl in Hollywood High, but we also played with dolphins together."

Were they this close when they first sat down? She didn't think so. Now their legs touched under the water, and Ricky's face was inches from hers. She knew she should move, but her heart anchored her firmly in place.

He reached up with a wet hand to touch her hair, using the same gentleness he had exhibited with Cocoa. "I love your hair like this. You've grown into an extraordinarily beautiful woman."

He cupped her cheek, the heat of his touch contrasted with the cool rivulets of moisture dripping down her throat.

Her heart beat so violently that she felt sure it would start a tidal wave in the tiny pool. She closed her eyes when his lips were less than an inch from hers. Instantly she was transported to another time, a similar situation. She was in that backyard pool with the boy who had become her best friend, the boy who gave her her first kiss.

His lips were as she remembered them, soft, sensitive—his breath warm and sweet.

"MISS BEFANY?"

With a splash, the couple pushed away from each other. Emily's mother stood near the pool in stunned silence holding the little girl's hand. Bethany felt her face sizzle with the water that had followed her hand.

Emily's mom stammered her apologies. "I—I'm so sorry. I shouldn't have let her burst in on you like that—but we were visiting, and Emily wanted to see you." She pointed weakly toward where they had just come. "They told us you were in here."

"It's okay." Bethany tried to recover. "We were having an interaction—that is—um—this was an encounter—I mean. . ." She took a deep breath and tried again. "How are you, Emily? I've missed you."

Bethany sloshed out of the pool and grabbed a towel. She knelt for a hug from the child.

Over Emily's shoulder, she saw Simon standing at the entrance. Had he escorted the two in? What had he seen? She swallowed hard and tried to force the blush from her cheeks.

"Bethany, when you're through, may I see you in my office?"

Strike two.

eighteen

"The answer is *no*. Look, I don't want to be difficult, but is there any way we can rework the dates?" Brick squeezed the cell phone as if it were the neck of the person on the other end of the conversation.

Daryl's strained voice sounded tinny with the weak connection. "I'll see what I can do, but this is a great opportunity to improve your image and promote the movie."

Brick caught a glance of himself in the mirror as he paced in front of the bathroom door. This image was not what the public wanted. And what did he want? Was he ready to put on the cloak of superstardom again and resume his career? He answered his own question when his pacing propelled him toward the bay window in the small guesthouse.

Bethy. She had decided to work in the garden after church. There she knelt, creating a portrait, framed by the white, wooden French doors leading to her father's office. Her feather-soft hair blowing ever so slightly, she looked like a dove resting near the azalea bush. He watched as she tenderly worked a yellow mum out of its container. With whimsy, he imagined himself as that mum. Little by little, she had been working him out of his tight container, the restraint of his past. But was he ready to be planted, allow his roots to take hold of something solid—Bethy's faith, for instance?

Daryl's voice drew him back: ". . .getting impatient. I don't know how much longer I can hold them off."

"Hey, if we miss this opportunity, it's no sweat. It's just a commercial."

"Just a commercial? This is *the* commercial. No one else can do this but you. This company gave you your start. A cameo of the now-famous Brick Connor would not only be good for you, but for the men's cologne and the movie. It's promotion all the way around."

Bethany must have noticed his movement in the window. She looked up at him, her genuine smile causing a sensation akin to a warm, healing oil that saturated his heart, a balm to his hurting soul. When he would come home from school to find his father waiting for him, he would remember that smile and couldn't wait to get back to its warmth.

"Daryl, just do what you can, okay? I plan to stay away for at least another month."

❧

After a week of rehearsals, all the players began to feel comfortable with one another. Ricky considered them family. The pastor named Gary looked the part of Jaques to the point of being comical. His basset hound eyes and jowls made him perfect for the morose lord of the banished Duke Senior.

"Gary," Judy called to him. "Have you memorized your speech?"

"Yes, ma'am," he drawled.

Judy called for all those in Act 2, Scene 7 to come forward. The scene progressed to verse 140, where Jaques took center stage. His droopy eyes drew heavenward as he began the famous speech.

" 'All the world's a stage, and all the men and women merely players: They have their exits and their entrances; and one man in his time plays many parts. . . .' "

He went on to describe the seven ages of man: The infant in the nurse's arms. The whining school-boy with his satchel, creeping unwillingly to school. Then the lover, sighing like a furnace. A soldier, full of strange oaths; then the justice, in fair round belly, full of wise saws and modern instances. The sixth age led into the lean and slipper'd pantaloon, an old man, with spectacles on his nose and his big manly voice turning again to childish treble.

Jaques wandered to stage left, scratched his head, and finished the speech. " 'Last Scene of all, that ends this strange eventful history, is second childishness and mere oblivion, sans teeth, sans eyes, sans taste," with a sweep of his hands, palm upward, he finished, " 'sans every thing.' "

"Well, Ricky." Gary's jowls flapped a little, even in his seriousness. "I often wonder how people handle life without God. I suppose that's the way they see it. But me, I know there is much more; in fact, it's just the beginning. I may end life sans teeth, eyes, and taste, but when my body gives up, my spirit will soar to heaven, and straight into Jesus' arms." Gary closed one droopy eye in a half wink and bore into the younger man with the other. "Do you believe that, son?"

Ricky smiled. Vince would have said the very same thing. He reflected a moment. Did he believe it? He searched his heart as Bethany had suggested. She and her family believed it, and he wanted to because that would mean her mom was in heaven. But if that were the case, where was his father? He felt a chill grip his spine. And if he had prayed the man to his grave, would he suffer the same fate?

Gary waited for an answer. Ricky shoved his hands into his pockets and shrugged. "I'm not sure I'm ready to believe it."

"What's stopping you?"

Dare he go into his past? Sure, he'd prayed a salvation prayer when he was a kid. But should he confess that he continued to have trouble relating to a loving God who would allow a child to be abused? And yet, the Hamiltons took him in and loved him unconditionally. Did God prompt them to do that? Did He care enough to put Bethany in his life?

In answer to Gary's question, Ricky cleared the lump in his throat. "I guess the jury is still out. I have some—issues—to deal with first." He rubbed the scar on his chin.

Gary smiled, which didn't improve his naturally sorrowful look at all. "That's what God is for, son, to deal with those issues for you."

Bethany skipped up to the two men and announced, "I'm ready."

Ricky grabbed the door handle. *But am I?*

nineteen

Had he heard correctly? *Surely not.* Ricky went in search of Bethany to ask if it were true. He found her pouring a bag of chocolate sandwich cookies onto a platter in the fellowship hall. The service that Sunday had been moving, but he confessed to himself that singing with Bethy in the choir touched him more than the sermon.

He waited impatiently for her to finish a conversation with a fellow choir member. The woman said, "Bethany, how domestic of you. Did you make those yourself?"

Bethany played right to the gathering crowd. "Why, of course. The trick is to not let the frosting in the middle melt."

When the hoots of laughter died down, Ricky leaned in and said, "I have to clear something up." She looked at him with a curious angle to her brows. He spoke barely above a whisper. "What's a mullet festival?"

Her mouth sprang open in surprise, and an errant giggle escaped her throat. "You're kidding, right?"

"Why would I kid about that? People keep asking if I'm *fixin'* to go, and I don't want everyone to think I'm dumb. Why would they have a festival to celebrate a hairstyle?"

This time, her giggle turned into an outright guffaw. He felt heat rise up his neck as she pulled him to a corner of the large room for more privacy. "It's not mullet as in *short in front, long in back*, silly. It's mullet as in the fish."

"Oh, that makes more sense." He sat on one of the long tables not currently in use. "I kept envisioning a large roomful of bad haircuts."

Bethany leaned her hip against the table he sat on. "They're talking about the annual Boggy Bayou Mullet Festival. It's held in Niceville—"

"Now you're kidding. There's really a place called Niceville?"

"Yes. Niceville, Florida. It's across the bay, a beautiful little town that hosts the festival every year. Mostly craft booths and good eating, but there's also entertainment—local and well-known. Dad's playing there next Sunday with the swing band; want to go?"

"Sure. Do I have to grow my hair long in back?" He shook his sandy tresses, and she slapped him playfully.

"Okay, you two, am I going to have to break you up?" Cleo closed in on the couple.

Ricky smiled. He knew why Bethany liked Cleo so much now that he'd gotten to know her. He glanced toward her swelling belly and remembered hearing she was five months along. "Hello, Little Mama. How are you feeling?"

Cleo blushed, turning her freckles into tiny pink dots. "Just waiting for the morning sickness everyone insists I should have. It was supposed to hit in the first trimester, so maybe I dodged that bullet. How are rehearsals going?" Then with a conspiratorial whisper, she asked, "No one's seen through the disguise, have they?"

Ricky lowered his voice, as well. "If they had, do you think I'd be sitting here enjoying *homemade* sandwich cookies?"

&

The week progressed uneventfully, much to Bethany's relief. While she enjoyed Ricky's presence, she still found herself constantly looking over her shoulder. Things were going much too perfectly.

The couple had asked Cleo to attend the festival with them.

"You sure I won't be intruding?" She gave Bethany a look that clearly translated *Give me the sign, and I'll back off*.

Bethany assured her that her presence was more than welcome, and she smiled when Ricky affirmed her stance.

They arrived at the festival, and Cleo asked, "Are we going to see your dad around? When's his group scheduled?"

"They play at five thirty, just before the main act."

"Who's the main act?" Ricky asked.

"I'm not sure. Some country-and-western band. I guess they're pretty popular, but I'm not into country."

Both Ricky and Cleo answered at the same time. "I know." They slapped each other's palms in a high five.

"You two think you know me so well." Bethany's heart felt full and warm as she laughed with her two best friends.

"Jazz and country in the same day." Cleo scratched her head. "Go figure."

"Well, this festival is known to be eclectic." Bethany sniffed the air noisily. "Speaking of. . ." She sniffed again, this time holding her finger in the air, using it as an odor barometer. "I smell Oriental, and Cajun, and barbecue, and. . ."

"And mullet." Cleo's freckles paled to an ashen gray. "I'm sorry, you guys, but morning sickness has finally arrived."

Ricky rushed her to a chair under the large food tent, and Bethany went in search of a cold towel.

She returned shortly. "Here. I managed to bum these wet paper towels from the gyro booth." She laid it over Cleo's already moist forehead and fanned her until some of the color returned. "Feeling better? The gyro guy offered ice if we need it."

"No, I'm fine, but only if you promise not to say the word gyro again." She took a small sip of lemon-lime soda that Ricky brought to her. "I think I'll stay here for a little while. Why don't y'all walk around? I'll just sit and listen to the music. When I feel normal again, I'll find you."

Bethany began to protest, but when Cleo insisted, she acquiesced reluctantly. Petting the strawberry curls, she said, "We'll only be gone a few minutes—just long enough to take in the craft booths."

"Go, I'm beginning to feel better already. Oh, look!" She pointed to the crowd. "There's Sheila looking for a place to sit. She can babysit me until you get back."

As they walked into the mob, Ricky said, "I love your loyalty. You're a good friend, Bethany Hamilton." He slipped his hand around hers, thrilling her to her toes.

"Cleo gives much more than she gets. I don't know what I'd

do without her. She's my rock. Or rather," she ventured to say, "Jesus is my rock through her." *Oh, Ricky. Let Jesus be your rock through me.* He squeezed her hand slightly, and she took it to mean that he was listening.

They did as they were told and perused the craft booths. They oohed and aahed over beautiful pottery, paintings, and metal sculptures. They laughed at quirky wind chimes, dolls, and toys. Ricky bought all three of them official Mullet Festival T-shirts, and Bethany bought the baby-to-be a handcrafted quilt.

Eventually they ventured upon a booth of seashell art. Ricky seemed particularly interested in one piece but kept Bethany from seeing it. He shooed her to another booth containing plant slips in hanging glass bulbs.

"I want to surprise you," was all he told her.

"The shirt is enough. You don't have to buy me anything else."

He put his hands on his hips and tilted his head. "Don't you think I can afford it?"

She laughed, as much at the incredulous idea as the picture he created with his body language. "Well, as long as you don't lose your home in Fiji."

He winked. "No problem."

She feigned interest in the hanging philodendrons and ivy until he joined her. He held out a bag, and she eagerly reached for it.

"Oh no, you don't," he said, pulling it back with a teasing sparkle in those beautiful green eyes. "It's all wrapped up."

"That's not fair," she mock-wailed. In truth, she'd rather open it at home, away from the crowd, alone with the man grinning in front of her. Her gaze flitted to the other booths. "I'd like to reciprocate."

"Let's call it a thank-you gift for putting up with me these last few weeks."

No, Ricky. Thank you.

He gathered the bags she'd been carrying and offered to take the booty back to the car. "I'll meet you at the food tent. Go check on Little Mama."

At the tent, she looked at the table where she'd left her friend and shook her head. "I don't believe this."

Cleo was exactly where they'd left her, but now she was surrounded by empty plates, napkins, and a large plastic cup.

"What? I got hungry."

&

When Ricky reached the tent, he, too, looked at Cleo in amazement. "How did you put away that much food in such a short amount of time, especially after nearly being sick?"

"It passed." She shrugged as if it were totally normal to be on death's door one minute and ravenous the next.

"Where's Bethy?" He looked around the area.

"She went to get some food." He raised an eyebrow. "Not for me. For you two. She wants you to try some of our local culinary delights."

Bethany showed up at that moment carrying a cardboard tray stuffed with plates from different booths.

"How did you carry all of that? I don't ever recall you working as a waitress." Ricky helped her unload.

"I played Dulcinea, didn't I? The serving wench."

Cleo interrupted. "Okay, Don Quixote, before you break into the chorus of 'The Impossible Dream,' sit down and take a whiff of this stuff."

Ricky looked at the—*what was the word?*—eclectic fare set before him. "What's yours, and what's mine?" He picked at the closest thing with his fork. It appeared to be some sort of meat.

"This is mine." Bethany noted a bowl of something murky. "Mullet chowder."

"Yum," he said with little enthusiasm.

Cleo's eyes danced as she pointed out another dish. "Try this one."

He took a tentative bite and promptly spit it out. "What is this stuff?"

"Smoked mullet," Cleo said.

"I don't think I'm a mullet man." He wiped his mouth and poked at another potentially lethal dish. Deciding against that one, he chose another. "This doesn't look too dangerous." It was a crispy-fried something on a stick. If it came on a stick, it couldn't be too bad, could it? He took a tiny bite, then a bigger one. "Now this is more like it." He ate a whole piece before he said, "This tastes like chicken."

Bethany and Cleo grinned at each other. Together they said, "It's alligator."

"What?" Ricky stood so abruptly that he bumped his thighs on the bottom of the table, nearly spilling the drinks.

Abandoning the feast laid before him, he went in search of a hamburger. Giggly girl laughter danced behind him, making him chuckle to himself.

After their meal, they walked around while listening to light swing music wafting through the festival. When the last note had wailed on Glenn's trumpet, they decided to see who the headliner was that evening. Out came three energetic women in cowboy costume and stringed instruments. Ricky looked frantically for a place to hide.

twenty

"Orange Blossom Special" erupted from the band, and Bethany started clapping along with the crowd. The redhead playing the violin was especially good, using her whole body to produce the energetic notes.

"Um. . . We're too close here." Ricky tried to pull the girls back into the pressing crowd.

"Are you kidding?" Bethany yelled, trying to make herself heard. She glanced toward the stage and was thrilled that she could practically see the color of the woman's eyes. "This is perfect."

The song ended, and Bethany looked back to say something to Ricky, but he had disappeared. She nearly tripped over a large mass huddled near the ground. "What are you doing?"

"Tying my shoe," Ricky said.

The band began another number. Bethany found herself enjoying the music. It wasn't as country as some she'd heard, and the harmonies of the women, as well as the musicianship, were outstanding. She turned to tell Ricky as much and found herself looking at the top of his head.

"I think I bruised my legs at the table earlier. I can barely stand." He hunched over and rubbed his thighs. "Would you mind if I slipped back and sat awhile?"

"Would you rather leave?"

Cleo heard the conversation and piped in. "You know, I'm getting pretty tired. I probably shouldn't be standing this much." Bethany looked into her friend's clear blue eyes to investigate whether Cleo was actually exhausted or just spoiling the pampered actor.

"Okay," she finally said, interpreting Cleo's heavy lids as the truth. "I can buy one of their CDs later."

As they prepared to leave, she noticed Ricky looking over his shoulder at the fiddle player onstage. That didn't bother her nearly as much as the way the musician looked back at Ricky—not in a flirty way, but with recognition.

❧

After Ricky dropped Cleo off, Bethany turned to him in the little car. "Do you want to tell me what that was all about?"

"What?"

"That exchange back there. At the festival?"

Ricky tried to feign an innocent look, but seeing the determination in Bethany's face, he knew he'd been busted. "Okay. That woman? The one playing the fiddle? She. . .um. . . kinda knows me."

He heard Bethany gasp. They'd just left Destin, where Cleo lived, and there were no more lights for a few miles. He didn't need to see her face. He knew she'd fear his cover was blown and be hurt he'd attempted to keep the truth from her. He didn't want to see that look.

"How does she *kinda* know you? Could she be a threat?"

He turned down one of the many roads that led toward the beach. They parked where they could see the full moon over the Gulf.

As he put the gears into PARK, he noted her crossed legs and arms. She'd already begun to shut him out. "Her name is Maggie Carter. I don't think she processed what she saw." At least he hoped not. "We dated recently."

"How recently?"

"Up until July."

"Of this year?"

He gripped the top of the steering wheel and nodded.

"So, you're saying, you and she were a couple while you were making your movie, while we were—getting reacquainted." The pain in her voice broke his heart.

"Bethy." She shot him a look that wordlessly objected to the use of that name. "I actually broke it off with her because of you."

"And this is supposed to make me feel better?" She tapped her foot on the floorboard. "How do they do it in Hollywood? Do I bat my eyelids and feel grateful that you chose me over her? Do I feel triumphant that I won such a grand prize? You tell me."

"Wait a minute." This little temper tantrum needed to be nipped in the bud. "I didn't know I was going to see you again. All I did was renew our friendship. Then," he said, softening his words, "when I got home, I realized Maggie couldn't compare to you."

He reached across the back of the seat and playfully tugged her short hair. She tried to ignore him, but a tiny uplift of her mouth betrayed her. Her arms unwound, and she placed her hands under her thighs.

"Now, I'm sorry." Then she became somber again. "Ricky, you've suspended your life for me, but what happens when it's over?"

"What do you mean? It never has to be over."

She opened the car door and walked toward the beach. Ricky followed, not sure what to expect. She stopped just short of the water. "Look out there, Ricky."

She folded her arms around herself as a crisp breeze suddenly snatched at her thin sweater. He took off his light jacket and wrapped it around her. She never took her eyes from the Gulf. "What am I supposed to look at, Bethy?"

"I'm a fish, and you're a bird. I can't live your lifestyle any more than you can live mine."

He looked out toward a dark cloud blanketing the water in the distance. Lightning lit it sporadically, reminding him of a florescent bulb about to go out.

Turning her shoulders to face him, he said, "Then I'll have to buy a snorkel." He wiped a tear from her cheek and placed his lips over hers. His heart pounded as she returned the kiss. She wrapped her arms around his neck and twirled his hair with her fingers, just as he remembered her doing when they were kids.

When it was over, way too soon in his opinion, she dipped her head and he kissed the top of it, reveling in the herbal scent of the feathery softness.

She looked up at him, and he didn't like what he saw in her eyes. "What about God?" she asked.

That again.

"I've told you: There's a lot of junk to sort out first."

"You've been trying to sort it out for years. It's beyond your capability. Talk to God; be honest about your feelings. He wants to take your pain away. All you have to do is let Him."

He broke away from her this time, a first in their new relationship. Should he tell her why he couldn't yield this to God? No, he couldn't dig that deep into the wound. She would see him for the ugly person he knew himself to be. He balled his fists and pressed them into his temples. The scar on his chin, though long healed, suddenly throbbed.

"What? Talk to me, Ricky." She touched his sleeve, and he again thought her fingers as gentle as butterfly wings—or was it angel wings? He couldn't handle the pureness of that image and started walking back to the car, but her next words stopped him in his sandy tracks. "Your father is dead. He can't hurt you anymore."

Without turning back, he ground out through his teeth, "But he does. He hurts me every day."

&

Bethany fell back across her bed. How could she allow herself to fall in love with him again? Had she never fallen out of love?

"Oh, God," she said, feeling her prayers weren't pushing past the ceiling fan. "Why have You brought that man back into my life? He's harboring unforgiveness, and it's hurling him down the wrong path. I can't have a relationship with him when I can see there will always be this hatred hanging over him. That can't be a healthy environment in which to bring children." Swiping at the tears flowing toward her pillow, she added, "What am I supposed to do? Take him by the hand and baby him?"

Willy padded onto Bethany's chest and tickled her hot cheek with stiff whiskers. With the pet's unique chirp, she soothed, using empathetic kitty language. Bethany buried her face in the silky neck and prayed, petitioning for Ricky once again.

The next day, Bethany went through the motions, but her heart wasn't in her work. After the last therapy session, she searched out Cleo. She needed a shoulder to cry on, and Cleo was the only one in on the covert operation. When she entered the gift shop, the assistant manager greeted her. Bethany looked around. "Where's your boss?"

"At home, sick."

Bethany's heart dropped. Had she allowed her to do too much yesterday? Why hadn't Cleo called? "I hope it's not serious. Is it the baby?"

"In a way. Just morning sickness. She called early to tell me she'd have to let it pass, but she'd be in this afternoon. I persuaded her to stay home and rest."

"Good." Bethany wandered out of the shop, feeling utterly alone.

That evening when Bethany arrived home, a candlelit dinner awaited her. A present with her name on it lay on the table, next to a dozen long-stem roses in a crystal vase.

Ricky entered the small dining room carrying a large bowl of creamy chicken Alfredo. The savory bouquet of Parmesan and oregano floated from the steam, and her stomach growled.

"Oh good, you're home." Ricky smiled, prompting her previous image of a househusband. "I hope you're hungry. Sit down, and I'll get the salad." He disappeared into the kitchen.

Bethany followed him, expecting to find takeout containers littering the countertop. Instead, pots and pans, cooking utensils, and various herbs and spices were evidence that someone had made a home-cooked meal.

Ricky pulled a tossed salad out of the refrigerator and turned to look at her. "You seem surprised."

"I didn't know you could cook. Since you've been here, you've either ordered out or grilled."

He took out a smaller bowl, stirred the contents with a wooden spoon, and poured them over the salad. Bethany cocked an eyebrow, and Ricky said, "My own concoction of oil, vinegar, and other stuff I'm not at liberty to divulge." He raised a brow à la Dan Danger. "Top secret, hush-hush stuff." He ushered a still-dumbfounded Bethany back to the dining room. "I've been a bachelor for a long time, Bethy. Did you think I lived on fast food?"

As he pulled the chair out for her, she wondered how he could bounce back so easily. When he'd left her the previous evening to retreat into the guesthouse, his feet dragged as if they were made of lead. She'd upset him, yet here he was, serving her a delicious meal. *Yes, Ricky, you are a very good actor.*

He scooted the present in front of her.

"Go ahead; open it."

In seashell paper tied with a golden ribbon, the box was too pretty to unwrap. "Did you do this yourself?" Thankfully, the gift was too big for jewelry. She opened the lid and found tissue paper wrapped around a square object. A beautiful shadow box lay nestled within the folds.

"I got it at the festival." He looked like a child giving his first girlfriend his favorite frog. "The lady said this is a real sand dollar."

Bethany stroked the round seashell with the tip of her finger. "We don't see too many here along the Gulf because of the sandbar off the coast. They get smashed to bits before they can make it to shore." But this one was broken on purpose. The two pieces were neatly arranged, and little shells in the shape of doves appeared to float out of it.

"She also said that sand dollars really do have these little doves inside them." Ricky pointed out each tiny piece. "A phenomenon, I guess."

A *ding* was heard from the kitchen. "My bread."

When he left, she counted each dove that had been glued to blue velvet. Five. Her eyes drew to two hovering near a piece of coral. The one nearest was Ricky, she mused, beckoning her to follow him, to take a chance. She frowned. Coral, although pretty, was sharp and could hurt you, just like the world into which he wanted to draw her.

You have it wrong.

This thought was clearly not her own.

The dove nearest the coral is you.

A peace settled over her. God had answered her rebellious prayer of the night before, giving her a clear directive to take Ricky by the hand and help him through the coral—or was it the world? Unscathed and unscarred.

And the other three doves? There was that voice again. *They are for your father, your mother, and your grandmother. All symbols of loss. They are free of the sand dollar and in My hands now, as are you.*

Large tears overflowed.

Ricky laid the bread basket on the table and knelt beside her chair, concern filling his eyes. "No, don't cry. Have I done something wrong?"

She embraced him and buried her face in his neck. After several moments, she finally managed to speak. "Ricky, this is the best present you've ever given me. I can't explain right now, but in these last few minutes, my life has changed." She placed her hand on his face. "Because of you." Then she kissed him soundly to assure him as well as herself that not even the storms of life would keep them apart again.

twenty-one

"Take five, everybody." Judy's stage voice projected from the third row. "Ricky, may I see you down here, please?"

Ricky reached the seats and plopped down next to the director, who had five pencils stuck in the band above her ponytail.

"Ricky," she began, "I've been meaning to discuss this with you. You're very good, and you have your role down pat, but. . ."

He tried to keep his amusement to himself. Upon reflection, he realized he was Ricky, playing Brick, playing Ricky, playing Orlando. The thought tickled him deep down, but he assumed a somber expression. "Have I done something wrong?"

"Oh no, I don't want to discourage you. Didn't you say you had acted onstage before?"

"In high school. Nothing professional, you understand." That was true; he'd never acted professionally onstage.

"I need more stage presence from you. Your actions are too tight. They need to see you in the back row."

"Okay." He nodded. It had never occurred to him before. He'd been trained for the screen. He played to the camera, where simple eye rolls and facial expressions were caught very easily. During close-ups, he'd been taught not to make big gestures, or he could find himself outside of the picture.

"I need more arm waving, more movement." Judy demonstrated with her notebook in one hand and her pen in the other. "Fill the stage with your presence, Ricky."

"Thanks. I'll try that."

He hopped back on the stage and played it big, almost feeling silly as he did so.

During the next break, Judy called them all together. "Remember, dress rehearsal Monday, Tuesday, and Wednesday. Opening night is Thursday. Bethany, I just received a beautiful wig that you'll wear in the beginning scenes until Rosalind becomes Ganymede. Then you will spend the rest of the play with your short-cropped hair, befitting a lady playing a boy."

Ricky leaned toward Bethany and whispered, "I don't think you could ever look like a boy."

"I wonder if I'll get a mustache."

"Hmm. I've never kissed anyone with a mustache before."

She placed her hand on his arm to draw him closer for what he hoped was a flirty remark when Judy's voice intruded.

"And, Ricky, I don't see Orlando with light hair. Think about dying your hair darker. There are products that wash out in just a few days." Judy went on to talk about costumes.

Ricky flinched. The affectionate squeeze Bethany had laid on his arm became a tourniquet-like grip. He knew what she was thinking. If he dyed his hair, his cover would be blown. He'd look too much like that actor Brick Connor. When had Brick become a separate entity? When did Ricky O'Connell insist on his own identity?

He looked at Bethany and saw the answer in her eyes. She wasn't in love with Brick. If anything, she was afraid of the film star. And for good reason. It had been Brick who let her down, who had forgotten about her. But Ricky would always be there for her. Always.

After rehearsal, Ricky managed to convince Judy, with Bethany's help, that Orlando's light hair symbolized his almost-childlike acceptance of Rosalind as Ganymede.

Performances played to a nearly packed house every night, and Ricky soaked in every sight, sound, and musky curtain smell. He could identify with Orlando, who in the opening scene confronted his brother for not providing him the education he felt he deserved after their father's death. Ricky also felt betrayed by the very family who trained him as an actor, then typecast him to a life of action and adventure films.

Then when Orlando met the fair Rosalind, Ricky could empathize. After her exit, his character lamented, "O poor Orlando, thou art overthrown!"

Orlando and Rosalind fled to the forest, him fleeing from his murderous brother, she in search of her father. Ricky and Bethany found themselves in a land not their own—Florida. He, running from his own fame. She, following her father.

When the mask came off at the end of the play, and Ganymede was proven to be Rosalind, she declared her love for Orlando. Had Bethany's masked feelings finally fallen away? Was their relationship back to where they'd left it?

How would it all end? Would Ricky and Bethany close with a kiss to a falling curtain? Was it true that *All's well that ends well?* He hoped so. The final performance was only a few days away, and he planned a very important announcement after the last curtain call.

ঽ৯

The weather early Sunday morning began deceitfully; the sun shone as if promising a bright autumn day, but dark storm clouds off the coast confirmed weather reports of yet another tropical storm churning over the Gulf. The Florida Panhandle would feel the effects around lunchtime.

Bethany sighed. She had met her quota of storms for the year. Especially those the weatherman couldn't predict—the torrents that drenched her heart. This one would hit several miles west, but it would drop enough rain to put a damper on their final matinee.

That morning, Bethany fidgeted through the service while struck with the knowledge that in a few short hours, she and Ricky would give their final performance. As the wind picked up outside, invading the century-old building, she swallowed a lump as she realized there would be nothing to keep him near her now. He would have to reenter his real life sooner or later. *Oh, God, please make it later.*

After hanging up her robe, she slid into her coat. They'd have to hustle to make it to the theater in time to put on their makeup and don their costumes.

She felt Ricky's hand on her elbow. His voice, that velvet voice, spoke low in her ear, "Is my fair Rosalind wont to take her leave so soon? Nay, may she roost in my heart forever as a gentle dove, and may she lend an ear to I, her feathered lover, who bids her a coo and a woo."

Bethany cocked her eyebrow, trying to look like a modern twenty-first-century woman but feeling very Elizabethan at his touch. "Smooth-talkin' words from someone who's more comfortable with a semiautomatic weapon than Shakespeare. And I don't recall that quote."

"Ah, milady. Thou hast brought out the poetry in this one, thy poor yet humble servant." He bent at the waist and drew her knuckles to his lips.

She withdrew her hand as if he'd placed hot coals on it. Casting a glance around the small music room, thankful they were alone, she cried, "Ricky. We're in public."

"I'll say you are." Cleo walked by the open door, laughing.

Bethany's cheeks warmed. "Uh. . .we'd better get going, Orlando. Curtain's going up in just a couple of hours."

"By your leave, milady."

"Stop that!"

The blustery wind assailed their hair and clothing as they stepped out of the church building. Huge drops of rain bombed the couple and the sea of umbrellas before them as everyone made their way to the parking lot.

"It's here," Bethany said, raising her voice.

They cinched their raincoats, but just as their feet hit the bottom step, cameras began flashing in their eyes. The numerous umbrellas weren't protecting churchgoers; they were hiding the dreaded paparazzi, those tenacious bloodhounds who had finally tracked Brick Connor down. They barked their questions at him and viciously tore at his privacy.

"What are you doing here, Mr. Connor?"

"Why have you changed your appearance?"

"Have you left show business?"

Bethany's worst fears were realized, until the umbrellas parted and she came face-to-face with a furious Maggie Carter.

twenty-two

The paparazzi eagerly made way for this new development. Ricky couldn't believe what or, more specifically, whom he was seeing. "Maggie! What are you doing here?"

"Interesting question, Brick." She spat out his name and ground it under her heel. "I think you should ask yourself that. The whole world has been wondering where you disappeared to. Now we know." Her glare bored into Bethany. "Is *this* what you left me for?"

Ricky pulled the trembling Bethany behind him. What must she be thinking with all these reporters in her face? A nightmare relived, most likely. He frowned at Maggie. "We had nothing, and you know it."

SLAP! Maggie's long musician fingers left a mark on the actor's face.

Bethany came from behind him with her teeth bared. She looked at the reporters. "All of you, leave him alone!" Ricky's mouth went slack. Was this his Bethy confronting the paparazzi?

He barely had time to savor that thought when he found Bethany thrust into his chest, caused by a brisk shove from the fiery redhead. Bethany grabbed at Maggie's arms, which were thrashing about like the winds from the storm that whipped around them. Ricky realized the singer was trying to rip out his ladylove's beautiful blond hair. He thrust his body between the two women, pinning Maggie at the elbows. Glenn, who had just barreled out of the church, held his daughter.

Ricky heard a strangled cry from behind his shoulder. He glanced at Bethany's pale face and followed the path of her startled gaze. A sporty rental car, not noticed in all the commotion, was parked along the street in front of the church. Chad Cheswick had stepped out and now strutted toward them like an arrogant peacock as he opened a black umbrella.

Ricky frowned at Chez. "Why are you here?"

Chez's face showed concern, but Brick knew there was something diabolical beneath that mask. "You're my best bud. I'm here for moral support."

There is nothing moral about you.

"I've been consoling Maggie ever since you dumped her."

Oh brother!

Ricky began to put the puzzle together. No doubt his breakup with the country singer made the news. Chez must have swooped in like a vulture to pick at the leftovers.

"You should have been more careful," Chez said with that insidious tone of concern. "When Maggie saw you here, she and I put two and two together. You wouldn't be the first man ruined by a pretty face." He grinned at Bethany. "Apparently, the news leaked." He spread his arms out to indicate the reporters hanging on his every word. "I'm sure your fans will forgive you for walking out on them. Your fling is over. Come home with us, okay, buddy?"

You slimy. . . "What are you talking about? Are you trying to make it look like I abandoned my career?"

"It's no secret how discontent you've been. I oughta know since we work so closely together." Chez turned toward the paparazzi, making sure they got his good side.

Questions were hurled at the actor from the sea of faces.

"Mr. Connor, is it true you've become jaded with Hollywood and plan to drop out for good?"

"Brick, what will you do now that your career is in the tank?"

Chez grabbed the hilt of the proverbial knife and twisted. He addressed the reporters. "Perhaps Brick has only been on a soul-searching mission." He looked at Ricky. "I see you're coming out of a church. Have you made peace with the father who abused you? Have you *found* religion?"

Tape recorders whirred. Cameras flashed.

Ricky gathered Chez's shirtfront in his fist. In low tones, he said, "I've never told anyone that. How did you find out?"

"We were drinking buds, remember? There was a lot of stuff spilled. Maybe you thought I was too fuzzy to remember. I kept your secret for a long time."

Ricky relaxed his grip. "Why tell it now? Are you that angry that Bethany likes me over you?"

The look in Chez's eyes finally revealed a true emotion. The sadness there caused a lump in Ricky's throat. "This has nothing to do with a girl. When did we stop being friends, Brick?"

His unspoken answer hit him square in the gut. Chez had become a victim to his fame just as Bethany had. When did his career take precedence over his relationships? Was he trying to lose himself in his work, hoping the past would disappear?

A reporter called out, "What did your dad do to you that made you run to God?"

Ricky thumbed the scar on his chin. With his defenses down, the child within, still mad at God, lashed out and answered for him. "No! I haven't found God because there is no God."

He'd suddenly tired of this game. He held his hand out to Bethany. "Come on. We have someplace to be."

When she shrank from him, only then did he realize what he'd said. She bolted down the steps and through the reporters.

"Bethy. . ."

Glenn grabbed his arm. "Let her go, son." He pulled him into the church and shut the door on the bloodthirsty rabble.

Maggie's muffled voice could be heard saying, "Did y'all know that Bethany Hamilton is Dee Bellamy's daughter? Might make a tidy side piece for this story, don'tcha think?"

ès

"Why didn't you tell us?" The pain in Judy's voice broke Bethany's heart. "The play went well with your understudies, but they didn't *wow* the audience like you and Rick—I mean, Brick—Oh, what do you call him?"

You don't want to know what I'm calling him right now. "I'm so sorry, Judy. It started out as an innocent experiment. We didn't mean to hurt anybody."

She hung up feeling as if she were the one who pulled the

curtain aside to reveal that the wizard was merely a con man. Last night, the phone calls began shortly after the news broke on *Entertainment, Now!* She didn't watch the program, but she heard all about it through friends from church, people in the play, and coworkers. She also knew that all of America, and worse, her community, knew she was Dee Bellamy's daughter. Her days of living a normal life were over.

With the stress of reporters camped out on her lawn, Bethany sat at the kitchen table having long abandoned the thought of breakfast. Instead, she simply sipped her soothing herbal tea as the memory of the day before pummeled her brain.

The phone rang, and her father yelled from upstairs that he would get it. Let him. She wasn't going to answer another phone as long as she lived.

Bethany's gaze wandered out the window facing the guest-house. Ricky had never come home yesterday. Did that mean he was out of her life forever? He'd promised that at the first sight of a camera he'd be out of there. She took another warm sip and managed to get it past the lump in her throat. She knew he didn't mean what he said at the church, but it still hurt. It hurt that they were back to square one, just when she thought they were making headway. She glanced at the wall where she'd hung the sand dollar gift. How would she lead him through the coral if he couldn't get past his anger?

Her father clomped down the stairs. When he entered the kitchen, his face looked as strained as she felt. "That was Simon. He doesn't want you to come in."

Bethany sighed with relief. "Fine by me. I could use the day off."

Her father sank in a chair beside her. "No, he doesn't want you to come in for a while. He wants you to stay away until things cool off. He thinks you'll be a distraction."

Strike three.

"Have you seen the paper yet?" he asked.

"Have you seen our front lawn?" *Snakes, all of them, coiled and waiting to strike with their cameras.*

Glenn stood and mumbled something while walking to the front door. She heard the click of the dead bolt. A mild hysteria rose in her throat, knowing that lock was the only thing keeping out the world. She heard the noisy questioning, like so many hungry seagulls claiming their meal. Then it stopped, and her father reentered the room.

"You're a brave daddy." She offered a shaky smile.

"I'm angry."

"With me?"

"No. With Simon. This is why he suspended you." He opened the *Northwest Florida Daily News* and flung it on the table. Bethany clutched at her heart to keep it from leaping out of its cage. On the front page was a picture of Maggie's hands reaching for Bethany's hair. But worse, Bethany's hands were reaching for Maggie's throat, or so it looked in the picture. She had actually been defending herself. The headline boasted LOCAL GULFARIUM DOLPHIN TRAINER IN OVER HER HEAD.

She felt her stomach churn. In the background, the sign above the door of Safe Harbor Community Church could be clearly seen: MAY ALL WHO ENTER HERE FIND PEACE.

&

"Room service."

Brick opened the door slowly. Satisfied the server was authentic, and alone, he granted entrance. After adding extra money to the tip to ensure the man's silence, he pulled the tray into the upscale room of the five-star resort, made possible through Glenn's connections. Bethany's dad had called a friend who'd provided a boat to take him from the church and away from the paparazzi. They sped away from the dock at the back of the church before the intruders knew what was happening.

Now he lifted the cover from the tray and took a long sniff of the ham and sausage omelet. He had already eaten everything in the minibar. That was yesterday. Today he would renew his low-carb diet and get back into shape.

While forking the warm eggs, yesterday's events came unbidden to his mind like they had all night. Before Bethany's tires had squealed out of the parking lot, he made a move to run after her, but Glenn's voice stopped him short.

Together they'd moved back into the church while the rest of the congregation kept the reporters out until the police could arrive. The two men sat in the sanctuary. Glenn's eyes looked weary, but they held compassion.

"You know I've always liked you, Ricky."

"Yes, sir. And you're the father I always wished I had."

"But I love my daughter and don't wish to see her hurt."

"Neither do I."

"I think you two could have a future if you just work at it."

What was he saying? "You mean, you still believe in me?"

"I've always believed in you, Ricky." Brick relaxed, as he always did when having these father/son chats with Glenn. "But you need to shed some old hurts, find some peace, and get on with your life. What you said out there hurt Bethany. Don't you see? She cannot and will not maintain a relationship with you until you've made peace with God. And only you can do that; she can't do it for you—no matter how hard she tries."

Brick's heart hardened. "But you saw what that monster did to me."

"Your father?" Glenn glanced at the scar. "Yes, I saw. Who do you think blew the whistle?"

Brick's eyes had opened for the first time in years. "You were the one who alerted the authorities? That tip is what gave my mom courage to stand up to him."

"I know, and don't think I didn't pray hard about it. I felt God leading me and probably should have called sooner. But see, God cared. He spoke to me, and I acted, albeit late. Sometimes that's how He works in our lives, by using other people. Did you expect lightning to zap your father where he stood?"

"That's what I prayed for."

Brick barely tasted his breakfast as he ruminated on that conversation. He knew God was real, despite his slip on the church steps, and that He had put the Hamiltons in his life.

How could I have gotten through childhood without them?

Apparently he couldn't do without them even now. Glenn had promised to pack his things in the guesthouse and bring them to him.

He looked at his watch. His flight would leave in a couple of hours; then he'd be going home. *Home.* Where was that exactly? Home was Bethy's arms. Home was in her eyes, and her welcome smile the hearth.

A complimentary newspaper had been brought with room service. Brick swigged the last of his tea, but at the sight of the front page, he did a classic spit-take as his unbelieving eyes saw his two girlfriends duking it out on the steps of Safe Harbor Community Church.

"Oh no. Poor Bethy." He knew what this would mean. She had predicted it correctly. Her ordered world would be shattered. He should have stayed away, but he had had to find out if there were still sparks between them.

It was as if they were still going steady at Hollywood High. As if her mother were still alive and he still sought refuge under their roof. . . Was Bethany simply a safe refuge for him? Or was she something more? He reached for the velvet box on the nightstand. The box containing the solitary diamond he had intended to give her after the matinee.

Something more. Definitely.

&

"Do you want me to come over?" Cleo's voice soothed Bethany's soul through the receiver. Her best friend had called her six times in twenty-four hours.

"No, the press would tear you apart." She sat in the mauve chair by her bedroom window. "The best friend of the home wrecker."

"They weren't married. How can you be a home wrecker?"

Bethany adjusted the phone between her shoulder and ear, then flicked the entertainment page of the paper with both wrists to straighten it out. "I quote, 'Brick Connor has dumped his soon-to-be fiancée, country singer and musician Maggie Carter, for local hometown girl Bethany Hamilton.' It quotes Maggie Carter as saying, 'That *home wrecker* has maintained, in her mind at least, a relationship with Brick for years. Finally her persistence has paid off.' Then it says that I cannot be reached for comment. Can you believe this trash?"

"No, and no one else who knows you will, either."

"Simon must. He's banned me from the Gulfarium indefinitely. He's afraid I'll be a distraction."

"I don't think Simon believes the press. He's just being protective of what is entrusted to him."

"You always see the good in others, don't you?"

"I try, but it's hard sometimes. Have you heard from Ricky?"

"You mean Ricky the deserter?" Bethany stood up with the cordless phone to pace her bedroom. "Ricky, the one who will come away from all this unscathed and more popular than ever? That Ricky?"

"Yes, that Ricky."

"No, and I'm so worried about him." She plopped down in the overstuffed armchair. Willy jumped in her lap and curled into a contented little ball. "I don't know if he meant what he said about God, or if he was just rattled. I'm feeling very guilty about my reaction, but he brought back memories of the old struggle. I don't think I can go through all that again."

"If you love him, you will."

"I don't know what I'd do without you, Cleo. You're so good for me. In return, I promise to spoil that baby rotten. I'll include her in our Girl Nights, and we'll teach her to have an appreciation for MGM musicals."

After a moment of dead silence, Cleo's voice cracked in Bethany's ear. She sounded unnatural when she said, "Is there any way you can sneak past the reporters?"

Bethany sat up, disturbing her kitty, which mewed in protest. "I guess I could go through the guesthouse and hop the fence into the neighbor's yard. She already called to see if she could help. Why?"

"Get some stuff together. I'll pick you up there. You're coming home with me for a few days. I have to tell you something, and I can't do it over the phone."

twenty-three

Bethany scribbled a hasty note to her father telling him where she'd be. While packing her overnight bag, she listened to the radio. The light jazz helped calm her spirit and gave her something else to think about.

However, the music was interrupted by a tinny voice from the National Hurricane Center. "Hurricane Olga is entering the Gulf of Mexico, where she will most likely strengthen. Those living anywhere along the Gulf Coast should take precautions."

Bethany continued to pack, discounting the forecast. She had other problems to deal with.

After an hour in Cleo's house, Bethany asked, "So, what did you need to say to my face?" She wondered if it had been just a ruse to get her out of the house.

Cleo squeezed Bethany's hands from across the kitchen table, her blue eyes brimming with tears. "Ed is getting out of the Air Force. We're moving to Colorado before the baby is born."

❧

Brick paced his Hollywood Hills home and picked up the phone for the twentieth time that day, and he put it down as he had the last nineteen times. Everything he could think of to say, he had said to the Hamiltons' indifferent answering machine. What more could he tell her?

He'd only been separated from her for a little over twenty-four hours. When no one answered earlier, he'd called the Gulfarium. Her father told him she'd been suspended and was most likely hiding behind the drawn curtains at home. So what else could he think but that she was avoiding him?

What was wrong with him? He knew how she felt about God. Then he went and blurted out such an insensitive thing. He didn't even mean it. Of course there was a God, but he was mad at Him for giving him such a rotten father.

He dialed the cordless phone again and listened to Glenn's recorded message. He tried once more to articulate some sort of apology, but the words wouldn't come out right. With a frustrated growl, he punched the OFF button and threw the phone at the sofa. After a muffled thud, it rang in seeming defiance.

Without checking the caller ID, he stabbed the TALK button and barked, "What?"

Dead silence greeted him. *Bethy?* But then a male voice disappointed him. "Having a bad day?"

"Oh. Hi, Vince. Yeah, you could say that." He sank onto the couch and rubbed the back of his neck.

"I heard about the scandal in Florida. How's our girl taking it?"

"I don't know. She won't talk to me."

"Give her time. Let things cool down. Once all this blows over, she'll come around."

"It goes deeper than that, Vince."

"You want to come over and talk about it? The wife made some awesome lasagna."

Brick briefly thought about his low-carb diet. "That sounds great. I'll be right over." *I hope she made a chocolate cake, too.* He grabbed his car keys. *With frosting!*

≈

"Chess?" Vince asked as they pushed away from the table, their protruding bellies evidence of a fine meal.

"Sure, but you'll probably beat me. My mind hasn't come back from vacation."

Vince brought out the chessboard with his prize collection of Shakespearean pieces. He chuckled. "It's still lying somewhere on the beach, eh?"

"Yeah." *Near a little town called Seaside, with Bethy.*

Throughout the first few moves, they made small talk. Each took turns moving pawns carved to depict Hamlet. Finally Brick worked up the courage to speak. "I can't give her what she wants, Vince."

Vince moved his knight, a small rendition of Nick Bottom from *A Midsummer Night's Dream,* complete with donkey's head. "And what does she want?"

"I guess a normal life." Brick countered with his knight. "I'm worth millions, but the one thing I can't buy her is normality." He nearly swore, but he'd only done that in front of Vince once. He'd never make that mistake again. "She could even have her own dolphin pool in our backyard."

Vince brought out his Friar Laurence bishop. "I could be wrong, but I think she'd take any life you'd give her if you'd only do one thing."

Brick also brought out his bishop, then realized he had been mirroring Vince's moves the entire game. He sat back in the leather wingback chair and pressed his eyes with cool and clammy fingers. "I've gone so long without contact lenses I have to get used to them again."

Great, Brick. . .avoidance. You know what Vince means.

He kept his eyes closed and thought about how far he'd slipped from those days in Bethy's youth group. Her presence made it seem easy. Even this last visit, he felt close to God. But now, so far away from her, he felt far from God, as well.

He heard the other chair creak and knew Vince had shifted his bulky body. When he opened his eyes, he had to smile at the villain of the *Danger* movies, gentle Vince, staring at the board, tapping his temple in contemplation of his next move.

Brick scratched the side of his nose. "You don't have to pretend I'm making this game hard on you."

"Thought I was a better actor than that." Vince's shaggy eyebrows rose with his twinkling eyes.

"I just know you well. You've been a great friend to me."

"I'm here for you, son; you know that."

Brick's throat closed. How he had longed for his father to say those words. A thought struck him so forcibly he flinched. *Have I been looking for a father figure all these years?* First Glenn, then Vince. He'd even warmed to Gary, the pastor who played Jaques in Bethany's play. If he could trust these men so easily, why couldn't he do the same with Bethy's heavenly Father?

"Vince?" Brick leaned forward and placed his elbows on his knees. He clasped his hands and stared at the Persian carpet on the floor. "I want the peace that you and Bethany have, but I think I've been avoiding a relationship with God all these years. She told me to be honest with God, but how do I tell Him. . ." Brick's voice cracked. "How do I tell Him about the murderous thoughts toward my father?"

"You don't think He knows them already?"

Brick's head snapped up to look in the compassionate brown eyes of his mentor.

"I have a favorite passage of scripture," Vince said. "It's from Psalm 139." Without taking out his Bible, Vince leaned back in his chair and closed his eyes. " 'O Lord, you have searched me and you know me. You know when I sit and when I rise; you perceive my thoughts from afar.' " He opened his eyes and looked pointedly at Brick. " 'Before a word is on my tongue you know it completely, O Lord.' "

Brick pulled out a handkerchief to stop the flow of tears. What was wrong with him? He hadn't cried since that night—that horrible night when he was sixteen. His mother had allowed Bethany to come over to share a pizza and watch a movie since his father was supposed to be out of town. He remembered preparing to pull out of the driveway to take his best girl home.

Suddenly a rough hand pulled him out of the car, away from Bethy.

"What is this, boy?"

Ricky had looked at the back fender. Where had that dent come from?

"I come back early, and this is the first thing I see?"

Searing pain pierced his chin as it hit the back taillight, splintering plastic and spattering blood. That hadn't hurt nearly as bad as hearing Bethany's anguished cry.

Dad had disappeared into the house. Apparently, splitting his son's chin was enough punishment. Ricky drove Bethany home—where he'd stayed, never to return until that monster was out of his house.

That night had been the first time his father drew blood and the first that Bethany had seen the violence. Later, through anguished tears, he'd vowed to her both would be the last.

"You can't change the past, son." Vince's soothing voice nudged him into the present. "But you can change the future. When you invited God into your life years ago, you became a new creation, but you held on to an old hurt. He already sees you as a new creation. If you let this go, you can finally say good-bye to the old person, the one who couldn't forgive."

Could it be true? God knew what had happened to him. God knew what he wanted to do in revenge.

Suddenly it all made sense. Glenn had told him, "I've always believed in you, Ricky. But you need to shed some old hurts, find some peace, and get on with your life."

When he'd told Gary he had issues to deal with, Gary responded, "That's what God is for, son."

And what was it that Bethy had said to him that day in her father's home office? "Look deep inside yourself. There's a big, black void in there, and only God's love can fill it."

And now Vince was confirming what he'd heard from each of these people.

O Lord, You have searched me and You know me. God had been with him through all of it; he knew that now. He put people in his life to ease the hurt. He gave him Bethany. Acknowledging that God hadn't abandoned him through the abusive years allowed the burden of his past to lift enough to where he felt he could breathe. *And, Lord, since You know me so well, You know I'll have a problem forgiving my father. But I want to, and I'll never be able to do it without You.*

Then Brick Connor, the Man of Danger, slid to his knees in Vince Galloway's study and rededicated his life to God.

twenty-four

"I can't believe this rain, and the storm is still miles offshore!" Another feeder band hit, and fierce wind caused Cleo's Volkswagen to swerve. Bethany watched the heaving surf out the passenger window of the little car. "I hope we get home before we're blown into the bay!"

The wind-driven pelt of rain forced them to speak louder.

Had it only been six days ago that the worst thing in her life was the paparazzi? Were her phobias ever as real as this? So what if people took her picture wherever she went? So what if her every move was reported? She'd trade this hurricane for all of that in a Hollywood minute. At least she'd be safe with Ricky.

"I wish we could have stayed put," Cleo said as she shifted gears. "But I don't trust that old house in hurricane-force winds."

"Last I heard it was a Category Four in the Gulf and heading east of Pensacola. We should be safe at Seaside." Bethany remembered her father saying that because it was a newer community the houses had been built to sustain heavy storms. "Better than getting in that long line of evacuees and risk getting tossed by a tornado."

❧

"We should have waited for your dad."

"I agree, but he told us to get home. He said he needed to finish boarding and overfilling the pools. I'm worried. Not only for him but for the animals. Can they do enough to safeguard them from a storm this size?" She prayed for her father's safety and that he'd make it home before the worst hit.

Almost to Seaside, they turned off the highway.

"What *is* that?" Cleo gripped the wheel and pumped the brakes.

Bethany screamed.

ɞ

Not even a week since his other life as Ricky, Brick threw himself into his work. He reviewed scripts for upcoming projects and researched possibilities for his new production company. He wouldn't allow himself a moment to think of the pain on Bethany's face.

Exhausted, he'd cleared his schedule for the weekend, beginning Friday afternoon. His heart wasn't in the Hollywood game anymore. He no longer needed to be seen at all the fancy bashes, all the premieres, and all the parties. Even before he reconnected with Bethany, he had begun to pull away from the fluff. Now he had a new problem. How would he put in the time to change his image, thus become more involved in his work, *and* convince Bethany that life with him would be normal—even low-key? His head hurt.

He grabbed the television remote, hoping to find something mindless.

"What?" He fumbled for the volume button. The weatherman pointed to a satellite image of the Gulf of Mexico. A swirling mass of clouds completely hid the vast body of water.

"Hurricane Olga has turned and is now expected to make landfall between Destin and Pensacola. Residents all along the Florida Panhandle as far as Seaside are beginning to feel the effects." Olga was heading straight for the Gulfarium— and Bethany.

ɞ

"It's going to hit us!" Bethany placed her arms over her face and braced herself for whatever was tumbling toward them on a blast of wind. She could feel the car jerk to the left, then right. Tires screeched as the Volkswagen spun out of control, like a spinning cup in the Mad Tea Party ride at Disney World. With a metallic crunch, they jolted to a stop.

Bethany sat in stunned silence, too frightened to move. Soon she felt Cleo's shaky hands stroking her hair.

"You okay?" Cleo asked.

Bethany blinked her eyes, trying to wake up from the

nightmare. She placed her palm on Cleo's stomach. "What about you and the baby?"

"We're fine. No pain." Cleo looked back at the road. "What was that?" She got out of the car. The passenger door was pinned shut by a scrub oak, so Bethany had to follow through the driver's side. A lawn umbrella had been the culprit, acting as a giant tumbleweed until it got caught in the brush.

Bethany shook her head. "Who would leave that outside in a storm?"

While watching for Glenn to pass by, they assessed the damage. The front fender had bent into the right tire. With rainwater streaming into her eyes, Bethany tried to pull it away, but with no success.

Tree limbs, plastic flowerpots, and other indistinguishable debris now swirled in the tempest.

"We'd better get back inside," Cleo said.

As they sat there dripping wet, assessing what to do next, the voice on the radio announced that Highway 98 would close within the hour.

"My dad! If he doesn't start for home soon, he won't make it. We'll be stranded." Bethany tried her cell phone. No signal. "The tower must be out."

They looked around. No cars or signs of life anywhere. They deliberated. Should they get out? Try to find someone home who hadn't evacuated? How close was the nearest neighborhood? Too far to walk in a storm. . . No, they were safer in the car—at least until they were either blown away or drowned in the storm surge.

Bethany felt a silent scream grip her throat. It made her voice sound thin and raspy. "What are we going to do?"

Cleo took her hand and bowed her head in prayer.

さ

"What do you mean there are no flights going that way?" Brick had become irrational. All transportation was heading out of Florida, not entering. Standby was the best they could do.

Local weather reports were sketchy at best. They didn't seem to care that Olga was about to finish what his ex-girlfriend had started—get rid of Bethany.

Brick lowered his head and launched into a prayer, still an unfamiliar act for him. "Dear God? Uh, Ricky here. Please weaken this storm. And watch over my girl, okay? Amen." As an afterthought, he tagged on, "Oh, and, God? If You help me get to Bethy, I'll never leave her again."

❧

Before Cleo could say "Amen," Bethany's father wrenched open the driver-side door.

"Are you girls okay?" Her daddy's face, stressed as it was with worry, never seemed so beautiful to Bethany. When they assured him they were fine, he said, "I just heard that the storm is weakening to a Category Two and beginning to break down, but there's a huge surge in front of her. Probably won't be that high this far east, but we still need to seek shelter."

He helped them out of the little car, and the three of them drove the rest of the five miles toward home. When they pulled into the driveway, Bethany's gaze searched her property. Not a camera in sight.

Nothing like a good, old-fashioned hurricane to blow away the garbage.

twenty-five

"Go fish."

"Argh! No way, Cleo. I thought you had a five." Now home and safe in a closet under the stairs, Bethany felt like a little girl at a slumber party, a battery-operated camping lantern their only light. Olga ranted outside, but among the heaps of pillows and blankets, she couldn't have felt safer. The radio reported the hurricane had lost its strength before landfall due to a wind shear and had dropped to a low Category Two.

Glenn, who had vacated the narrow space under the stairs long ago, peeked in. "Looks like we fared pretty well. No leaks inside. What I can see outside, there's debris everywhere, but I think the house is okay. I'll know more in the morning." He looked at his watch. "Wait a minute, it is morning. You girls can go upstairs to bed now; the worst is over."

Bethany tilted her head in the way she used to whenever she wanted her own way. "Aw, Dad. Do we have to?"

Glenn poked his finger into her left dimple and said, "That still works, tadpole. Just keep it down to a dull roar, okay?" He looked at Cleo, tugged the pigtail that Bethany had braided, and said, "As for you, little one, we'll look at the damage to your car and check out your house as soon as we can get through."

He disappeared, and Cleo poked her finger into Bethany's dimple just as Glenn had done. "Tadpole?"

Bethany tugged the pigtail. "Little one?" That launched both of them into a fit of giggles.

From upstairs, they heard "Keep it down!" To which they giggled some more.

Cleo finally lay down, her six-month pregnant belly protruding up. "Oh, that feels good on my back. Why are we so giddy?"

"Adrenaline, I guess." Bethany also stretched out. "We were terrified; now we swing the other way into happy oblivion."

"I wish I could call Ed. I'm sure he's worried."

"Hopefully it won't be long before the phone lines are back up working."

Is Ricky worried about me? She wrinkled her nose. He was probably so caught up being Brick Connor again that she doubted if he'd given her a second thought.

The two friends lay there in silence for a moment, coming down from the adrenaline high. Just when Bethany thought Cleo had fallen asleep, she heard "Beth, what are you going to do now?"

"What do you mean?"

"What if you don't have a job to go back to?"

"Don't say that."

"Seriously. Even though the storm hit farther west than anticipated, I'm sure the Gulfarium suffered damage. We should prepare ourselves."

Bethany swallowed back a lump. She had prayed for her sweet dolphins and the other animals off and on for the last twelve hours. "I suppose, if Simon will let me, I'll help clean up. I'm sure he won't refuse an extra pair of hands."

"But what if it takes a long time? Will you relocate to continue in another therapy program?"

Bethany sighed. Sometimes her friend could be as persistent as a cricket.

Cleo rolled over on her side and rearranged the numerous pillows surrounding her. "I'm just wondering, after everything you've gone through this week, if you've given any thought to your future."

Bethany reflected on Cleo's questions. It wouldn't be long before her father remarried, a fact she could finally embrace. Bethany would be a fifth wheel, so if she still had her job, she should probably move out. If not, maybe she could move back to Orlando and work at Sea World.

A soft, fluttery sound came from atop Cleo's pillow. Bethany marveled at how fast her friend had fallen asleep. Tears sprang to her eyes. She reached out and gently moved a stray strand of strawberry hair from the freckled face. *What am I going to do without you, Cleo?* This diminutive woman answered the child's cry within her that only a mother could silence. How typical that Cleo would have brought up her future. She must have wanted her *little girl* to grow up.

Bethany turned off the light and quietly left the closet. She tiptoed upstairs to the sanctuary of her room. Two glowing green marbles floated in the dark, and she heard a questioning "Mew?"

"It's okay, sweetheart." Bethany used the cat's eyes as a lighthouse in the sea of darkness to find her bed. She lay down next to the warm feline, nesting her within the curve of her body and stroked her to sleep.

"I don't know what I want to do, Lord." She peered into the darkness, barely able to distinguish her furniture. This was her future—obscure and murky. Her favorite psalm sprang to her mind, as if God had placed it there Himself. She began to recite. "'O Lord, you have searched me and you know me.'" God knew her better than she knew herself. That thought comforted her.

He taught her one thing this week. The paparazzi weren't nearly as scary as she'd remembered from her childhood. Annoying, yes, but compared to nearly riding out a hurricane in a Volkswagen, those flashing bulbs were nothing more than pesky bugs. And she knew now she had the strength to swat them.

She also learned that she loved Ricky so much; when he was no longer near her, her heart wept. Through her closed eyes, she could see the sand dollar doves hovering near the coral. "You promised that I would help him through the world, Lord. How can I do that if he remains *of* the world?" A peace washed over her as she felt God's answer. Ricky would be okay.

Another verse from that psalm played in her mind. *"If I say, 'Surely the darkness will hide me and the light become night around me,' even the darkness will not be dark to you."* The tears fell freely. Her future may be murky to her, but her loving heavenly Father could see it. Darkness was not dark to Him.

"Thank You, Father, for taking my hand, just as I'm to take Ricky's, and leading us together through the coral."

The next afternoon, after towing Cleo's Bug back to the house with Glenn's SUV, the phone rang and startled them all. Bethany answered, hoping to hear a velvet voice on the other end. However, it was Simon, so she promptly handed the phone to her father, not ready to talk to the man who had suspended her.

From Glenn's half of the conversation, she gleaned that the coast from Fort Walton Beach west toward Pensacola had sustained most of the damage. But east, Highway 98 between Destin and the Gulfarium had fallen victim to a twenty-foot storm surge that broke it to pieces and washed much of it into the bay. It would be months before they could drive to work.

"I'd like to check out the damage. How about by boat? Mine did pretty well in her slip. . . . Yours didn't? I'm sorry. Why don't I pick you up at your dock? Uh, you do still have your dock, don't you? Good. I'll be there in a few minutes."

Bethany decided to go, too. She had to see for herself how her dolphins fared. She hugged Cleo and apologized for leaving her.

"It's fine," her sweet friend assured her from the sofa, where she and a contented cat curled up together. "Get going and be back before dark."

Bethany kissed the top of Cleo's head. "Yes, Mom."

She hopped into the runabout while her dad started up the motor. The two putted away from shore, Glenn navigating carefully while watching for debris.

They pulled up to the dock where Simon was waiting. Bethany, who chose to sit in the back of the boat, stared in shock at the damage the storm had caused along the shore.

Simon stepped into the bobbing craft. "Sure glad you thought of this, Glenn," he said. "I didn't know how we were going to get over there."

"Sorry about your boat," Glenn said as he maneuvered back into open water.

"I should have tied her better, I guess. Hopefully she'll show up somewhere near here."

"Looks like you got it worse than we did."

Bethany surveyed the coast. Such devastation. Trees, littered about like pickup sticks, lay scattered about a small yacht that had been tossed yards from the water.

She hadn't said a word to her boss since he'd boarded the craft. The callous suspension still stung. Simon turned aft to face her, his greeting stilted. "Hello, Bethany."

She pulled her gaze from the shore. "Simon." She sat tall, lifting her chin. He may have bruised her, but he hadn't broken her. She wanted him to see that.

"I'm glad you're here," he said.

"Are you?" She raised a brow.

He drummed his knee with his fingers. "I can see that you're not going to make this easy."

"What?" she asked with a flash of anger.

"I'm trying to apologize." He let out a frustrated growl. "I'm sorry I suspended you. This storm has changed my priorities. And, well, I think I was unfair to you. We could certainly use your help cleaning up. And your job will be waiting for you when we're up and running again."

Bethany folded her arms. "I accept your apology, but my priorities have changed, too. I've decided to go back to school. I want to help abused children in the same way Sheila helps special-needs kids."

Her father spoke over his shoulder. "You never told me. When did you decide?"

"I had a long talk with God last night. He made me realize that I haven't truly sought His guidance. I know now I can't live at home forever. It's time for me to step out on my own."

She couldn't see her father's reaction, but she saw admiration in Simon's face. "I'll support that decision, Bethany. And if you need anything, please ask."

A weight fell from Bethany's shoulders. She'd never realized until then how much Simon's opinion meant to her. Suddenly she could see herself in his eyes. She realized he had never been antagonistic toward her for the sake of being mean. He simply couldn't trust her because she hadn't fully committed to his life's passion. Now that she had a goal, she imagined he could see her as an equal.

About a half mile from their destination, Bethany spotted a large gray mass on the shore. "Daddy!" She grabbed his shoulder. "Pull over there. I think it's a dolphin!"

ə

After finally getting a flight to Pensacola, the closest he could get to Seaside, Brick drove east along Highway 98. Seventy-two miles lay between him and Bethany. He pressed the accelerator of the rented SUV, his vehicle of choice when big buddy Vince had decided to tag along.

They had no concept of what a hurricane could do. If it had weakened, how bad could it be? They soon found out when they were stopped at a roadblock.

"I've got to get through. It's very important." Brick leaned out his window to talk to the uniformed man directing traffic onto a side street.

"Sorry, sir. Just keep bearing left." He continued to swing his arms.

"You don't understand. I have to see if someone is okay."

"To my knowledge, everyone along this strip evacuated. Now move it along."

Brick flung open his door. Horns blared behind him. Someone yelled, "Get out of the way, you moron."

He ignored Vince's warning to get back in the car. The Man of Danger, who had left home that morning in disguise, took off his hat and glasses and squinted at the officer's now-fuzzy frame. "Do you know who I am?"

The policeman tipped back his cap. "Yes, sir, I do know who you are, but if you were Sean Connery himself, I couldn't let you through. There are boats on the highway."

Brick and Vince looked at each other and mouthed *Boats on the highway?*

Brick meekly got back in the car and turned left onto the side street.

≈

"Is it one of ours?" Bethany leaped from the boat and swam toward the beach. *Oh, God, please let it be alive.*

Glenn anchored the boat while Simon grabbed a bucket and several towels from under the bench seat. By the time they joined Bethany, she was on her knees near the mammal, speaking softly to calm it. She looked up at them as they laid the wet towels over the sunburned body. "I don't know this dolphin. She's wild."

The animal's plaintive, high-pitched cry broke Bethany's heart.

They poured buckets of water over the towels they had draped over the large body, being careful to avoid the blowhole. Glenn began digging under the dolphin to help relieve the weight of her body on her lungs. But they needed to figure out a way to get her back in the water. She must have been about four hundred pounds—much too heavy for the three of them.

Before Bethany could finish her prayer for help, she heard an amplified male voice. "You, on shore, do you need help?"

The Marine Patrol!

Glenn stood and cupped his mouth. "We need a large blanket for a sling, and every man on your boat."

≈

Brick glanced toward his friend's sleeping form and felt a stab of guilt. He blamed himself for dragging the big man along, even though Vince insisted he was needed to keep him out of trouble.

They had been rerouted down Interstate 10, taking them thirty miles out of their way. At least they didn't have to go all the way to Seaside. His dogged phone calling finally paid off, but it was Cleo who answered Bethany's phone. She told him that Bethany and her dad had just left for the Gulfarium.

He turned off the interstate, praying that the road had been cleared. Traffic moved smoothly, but he noticed off in the thick-forested area that pine trees had been snapped, as if a large, angry child had grabbed at them in a tantrum.

Vince woke up as the SUV began its ascent onto a bridge spanning a large bay. "Where are we?" He yawned and rubbed his neck.

"We just left a town called Shalimar. This looks familiar. I think if I follow this street it'll get me to the Gulf. Bethany took me the opposite way to the mullet festival."

"Mullet?" Vince asked as he ran his hand over his hair.

"Don't ask."

Another roadblock created yet another detour. Brick slapped the steering wheel. "I can't believe this. I have all this money and clout, and I can't go ten miles to be with the girl I'm going to marry." Vince's shaggy eyebrows shot up on the last word. Brick scowled at him. "What?"

In the distance, they heard *wop-wop-wop*. They each leaned out their windows in time to see a helicopter fly overhead.

Brick grinned as he positioned the steering wheel for a U-turn.

"Follow that chopper!" they said in unison.

twenty-six

"Easy, girl." Bethany continued to talk to the dolphin as she poured water on her scorched skin. She wanted so much to take the lady back to the Gulfarium and treat her sunburn, but from what she could see, the Gulfarium looked like it needed saving itself. The entire beach had blown north and now spilled into the park.

A small boat powered toward them. Bethany squinted. "It's Tim!"

Tim Grangely pulled the motor-powered dinghy close, anchored, and leaped in to help.

"How are the animals?" Simon asked, his voice raspy with uncharacteristic emotion.

"It's a miracle. They're all alive. There's a lot of sand in the pools, but not enough to harm them. But," he said shaking his head, "there's so much destruction. It's going to take us months to get the place up and running again, probably years before we're 100 percent."

Months? Years? Bethany resolved then to stand good on her word. She'd help with the cleanup, but she knew her future was not at the Gulfarium, or with her father. She didn't know how she would do it, but she was going to learn how to help kids like Ricky.

She swallowed hard, suddenly realizing that her dream would have no meaning if he weren't in her life. She wanted him back, and she would make it work.

❧

The helicopter landed in a high school stadium. The two actors ran up to the pilot, who was helping a couple step out of the aircraft. The pilot, a middle-aged man who sported a black ball cap that read POW/MIA—NEVER FORGET, explained that

168

he'd offered his touring service to island residents to see how their homes had fared. But this had been his last run.

Brick presented his case.

The reluctant pilot squinted toward the west at the sun, almost at eye level. "Well, if it don't take too long. Sun'll set within the hour. Soon it'll be too dark to see anything, anyways."

As the two actors climbed into the helicopter, Brick offered the man money, but he refused it. "Nope, I done this for the displaced families free of charge; I can do it for love." He grinned, grabbed the stick, and lifted the bird off the ground.

Brick looked out the open door and down at the devastation. Houses were missing roofs and walls, furniture was scattered about, and boats were dry-docked on asphalt parking lots.

When the sound came into view, the pilot circled an object in the water.

"Hey, boys, you gotta see this."

"Is that what I think it is?" Vince hollered from the back to be heard.

"Yep, it's a house. Yessir, that Olga sure pushed a lot of water in front of her."

Brick could see the thin strip of island that separated the sound from the Gulf. It stretched for miles, barely a bump of sand in the water. Houses built on it were sure to be vulnerable.

"Matthew 7, verses 25 through 27." This was Vince's contribution. At Brick's questioning look, he raised his bushy eyebrows. "Look it up later."

The pilot shrugged and pointed the stick up the coast. Brick pointed to a large shell of a building. "What was that?"

"Five-star resort. Totally demolished."

Brick blinked back tears. It was the hotel where the benefit had been held—the same one where he had sought refuge from the media. How long ago was that? Not even a week? Now it looked like a bomb had blasted every floor in the place.

"We're coming up on your place."

Brick saw what had been the Gulfarium. White sand had infiltrated nearly every crevice. Atlantis must have looked like that, just before its final descent into the sea.

He looked around for Bethany, but the whole place seemed vacant. "Can you put us down over there?" Brick pointed to a flat area on the beach, where the dunes had been.

"No can do. I have strict orders not to land."

"I'll pay you."

"No amount of money is worth losing my FAA license."

They hovered over the area a moment longer. The bench was gone that had looked out over the Gulf, the place Bethany had first told him to stay out of her life, but also where she clung to him after the Chez fiasco. The roof to the Dolphin Encounter Building had been sheared back, and if he used his imagination, he could almost see where they had shared that first kiss—well, the first in this decade.

Where is Bethy? Maybe she'd already been there. Should he ask to be taken to Seaside? The sun was beginning its dip into the Gulf of Mexico.

"Mr. Connor, we've got to be heading back. I've pushed it too far as it is."

Brick nodded. But as they swung around, he noticed a flurry of activity about a half mile to the east. "Can we just see what that's about? They may need our help."

The pilot adjusted his hat, then grasped the stick and pointed the nose eastward.

"Look!" Brick yelled as he pointed. "There are boats and people on the beach."

"That's the Marine Patrol," the pilot shouted. "What are they dragging into the water?"

Brick's heart hammered in his chest. "It's a dolphin. And that fair-haired angel with the bucket is the reason I'm here." That was so true. If it hadn't been for Bethany's love and prayers, no telling where he would be today. "You've got to land."

"With the Marine Patrol there? No way!"

Brick glared at the pilot. "Hover as close as you can. I've got to see her."

"Okay, but I'm not setting it down."

❧

The rescue crew had almost freed the dolphin. Bethany continued to pour water over the towels. With the makeshift sling, the Marine Patrol maneuvered the dolphin to shallow water, taking it slow to keep from injuring her further. Simon had already examined her to the best of his ability without equipment and found nothing to concern him other than the sunburn. If they could get her into open water, she'd heal eventually.

Wop-wop-wop. Everyone looked up to see an approaching helicopter.

"What is that fool doing?" Simon asked. "Those blades are churning the water. Our girl is distressed enough." He patted the dolphin protectively, then started to wave the aircraft away.

Bethany caught his arm. "Wait! It's Ricky!"

Out of the gaping opening, Ricky leaned precariously. Their gazes locked. Her heart flipped when he smiled and waved at her.

She cupped her mouth and yelled, "Meet me at my house."

He cupped his ear and mouthed, "What?"

"He can't hear you," Simon said as he shook her shoulder. "Wave him away. You'll figure it out later."

She caressed the tiny-chip diamond on her left ring finger. *No.* She'd never tell him to leave again.

❧

"They want us to leave, Mr. Connor. We're disturbing the rescue."

"Brick." He felt Vince's hand on his shoulder. "We've got to go."

Brick took off his glasses and handed them to Vince. As he unbuckled his seat belt, he asked the pilot, "How far above the water do you think we are?"

The pilot's face went white. "I don't know. Twenty, maybe thirty feet. Listen, you aren't planning to—"

"Meet you in Sydney," Brick told Vince. Then he turned to

the open hatchway and prepared to swan dive.

He felt Vince's meaty hands grab his shirt to pull him back.

"Who does he think he is?" the pilot's voice squeaked.

Vince answered, "Agent Dan Danger."

❧

"Who does he think he is?" Simon frowned, clearly perturbed.

Glenn answered, "Agent Dan Danger."

Bethany wanted to close her eyes but couldn't. She knew what he was about to do, and it frightened yet thrilled her all at the same time. He was doing it for her. *But if he breaks his neck, what's the point?*

She finally took a breath when she saw Vince pull Ricky back into the aircraft. *Lord, please protect my impetuous man!*

To her dismay, the helicopter turned and headed west.

"Finally," Simon said. "Now let's get this lady back into the water."

Bethany continued to keep the dolphin wet but watched the vanishing dot in the sky disappear behind the Gulfarium rubble. Knowing they'd get together eventually did nothing to stop the growing lump in her throat.

The group finally freed the dolphin from her sandy prison, and she floated in the shallow water gaining her strength. All the humans did the same.

"Man," a Marine Patrol member said while catching his breath. "You guys do this every day?"

"Thankfully, no." Simon patted the large mammal. "But we've had our share of rescues."

Rescue. As Bethany listened to their conversation, the idea God had given her the night before finally gelled, and she now knew how she could continue her marine work and rescue abused teens.

"Dad." She turned to Glenn. "Do you know if Marineland has been sold yet?"

He looked at her quizzically. "I don't think so."

Wop-wop-wop.

Like the scene in a movie, the helicopter suddenly appeared

over a storm-battered hotel down the shore and sped toward them.

Bethany had to grin at her action hero, looking very Dan Dangeresque while holding firmly to a rope ladder several feet below the helicopter. But she had to remind herself that as an actor he'd done this many times with his own stunt work.

"Doesn't that guy ever give up?" Simon placed his hands on his hips.

"Nope, that's how he's survived all these years."

The aircraft slowed to a hover just in front of them, allowing Ricky to drop the short distance to the white sand still wet from the storm.

The ladder was quickly drawn up, and the helicopter made a circling path around them. Ricky looked up and waved at Vince, who could be seen grinning from the back passenger seat. He waved at Ricky, mouthed what looked like "No worries, mate," and then gave Bethany a thumbs-up. What had he said the night of the benefit? When Ricky finds his way back, God and all His angels would give her a big thumbs-up?

She blew Vince a big kiss.

The dolphin pulled away into deeper water, and Bethany knew her job there was done.

She sloshed her way toward the shore as Ricky closed the gap between them, wading into the water as if he couldn't bear another minute of separation. Feeling the same, she leaped into his arms, sealing their future together. She pictured their kiss on the silver screen and knew no other reunion moment could compare to their real-life romance.

"Bethy," Ricky said when they finally parted, "I have something to tell you. I've made my peace with God. I'm on my way to forgiving my father."

"I know; Vince just told me."

"Huh?"

She squeezed his hand. "I'll tell you about it later." Then she led him to the shore and thanked God that He had seen them both safely through the coral.

epilogue

"This is Bebe Stewart of *Entertainment, Now!*, reporting on Hollywood's golden couple, Brick Connor and wife Bethany.

"Godinall Production Company, Brick's pet venture, is actively seeking scripts dealing in social issues with messages of hope. No more *Danger* movies for this guy.

"Mrs. Connor's project will be unveiled next month. The Seaside Adolescent and Animal Facility for the Endangered is located in Los Angeles on a newly renovated lot where Marineland used to be. In a recent interview, Bethany had this to say: 'SAAFE is a place for abused teenagers to learn about the care of injured marine mammals and help them return to the wild. In a win-win situation, the mammals love the kids unconditionally. Plans to open a facility in Florida are now underway.'"

Bethany glanced at Ricky, snuggling the baby with his man-sized arm while channel surfing with the other. Just a week old, and Deedee was already beginning to look like her namesake, Grandma Bellamy.

Bethany joined them on the couch and took the television remote away from Ricky.

"Hey," he said, reaching for it playfully. "Never mess with a man and his TV."

"I'll trade it for the baby."

He wrapped both arms around the child and nuzzled her fuzzy head. "No way."

"It's late, and our Hollywood starlet needs her beauty sleep." She kissed his pouty actor lips and contentedly breathed in the scent of his cologne mingled with baby powder.

Before pressing the OFF button, she heard "Mother and baby are doing fine. This is Bebe Stewart, reporting your *Entertainment, Now!*"

A Letter To Our Readers

Dear Reader:

In order that we might better contribute to your reading enjoyment, we would appreciate your taking a few minutes to respond to the following questions. We welcome your comments and read each form and letter we receive. When completed, please return to the following:

Fiction Editor
Heartsong Presents
PO Box 719
Uhrichsville, Ohio 44683

1. Did you enjoy reading *Merely Players* by Kathleen E. Kovach?
   ❑ Very much! I would like to see more books by this author!
   ❑ Moderately. I would have enjoyed it more if

   _____

   _____

   _____

2. Are you a member of **Heartsong Presents**? ❑ Yes ❑ No
   If no, where did you purchase this book? _____

   _____

3. How would you rate, on a scale from 1 (poor) to 5 (superior), the cover design? _____

4. On a scale from 1 (poor) to 10 (superior), please rate the following elements.

   ____ Heroine   ____ Plot
   ____ Hero   ____ Inspirational theme
   ____ Setting   ____ Secondary characters

5. These characters were special because? _____

_____

_____

6. How has this book inspired your life? _____

_____

_____

7. What settings would you like to see covered in future
   Heartsong Presents books? _____

_____

_____

8. What are some inspirational themes you would like to see
   treated in future books? _____

_____

_____

9. Would you be interested in reading other **Heartsong
   Presents** titles? ☐ Yes ☐ No

10. Please check your age range:
    ☐ Under 18   ☐ 18-24
    ☐ 25-34   ☐ 35-45
    ☐ 46-55   ☐ Over 55

Name _____

Occupation _____

Address _____

City, State, Zip _____